Songs My Mother Taught Me

Songs My Mother Taught Me

Audrey Thomas

Talonbooks Vancouver 1993

Published with the assistance of the Canada Council

Talonbooks
201 - 1019 East Cordova
Vancouver, British Columbia
Canada V6A 1M8

Typeset in Goudy by Pièce de Résistance Ltée., and printed and bound in Canada by Hignell Printing Ltd.

First printing of the second revised edition: September 1993

Canadian Cataloguing in Publication

Thomas, Audrey, 1935 -
Songs My Mother Taught Me

ISBN 0-88922-329-7

Title.
PS8539.H62S6 1993   C813'.54   C93-091343-4
PR9199.3.T56S6 1993

Songs My Mother Taught Me: A Brief Reflection

In 1965, when I was living with my family out in Ghana, I had a story published in the *Atlantic Monthly*. This event quite literally changed my life. I had been very ill and, after that, very depressed for months. I remember sending that story off, not with my usual heart-fluttering optimism, kissing the brown envelopes for luck as I shoved them in the mailbox (I'd been writing stories for as long as I could remember, sending them away for several years), but with a kind of awful desperation — just to get the story out of the house. I was amazed when it was accepted — even more amazed when, after the story was pub-lished, both Edward Weeks, editor of the *Atlantic* (and with connections to Atlantic Monthly Press) and Bob Amussen, then editor-in-chief of Bobbs-Merrill, wrote to me.

Atlantic Monthly Press, it appeared, was very keen to see a book-length manuscript. Like Bobbs-Merrill, they were more interested in the idea of a novel than a collection of stories, but were enthusiastic nevertheless. I remember they said my writing reminded them of "Katherine Mansfield or the early James Joyce." While this letter was one of the items lost when a packing case went missing on our way back from West Africa, by then those words were burnt into my brain. Bobbs-Merrill went one better: they said "We'll agree to do a book of your stories if you will agree to do a novel later on." They sent me a contract which I was afraid to sign — it sat on my desk for days. I still wasn't well; I had two very young children; we were going back to Canada in the autumn of 1966. How would I ever manage to write a novel? Novels were written by men in "dens" or "studios," who only emerged when dinner was ready. ("Shh. Daddy's working.") I didn't know, then, that Harriet Beecher Stowe had had masses of kids — eight I think — and wrote at the kitchen table, just as I did back home. I didn't know, then, about Alice Munro living just across the water from Vancouver, where we lived, writing away like mad even if she didn't have money and a room of her own. There was a lot I didn't know about women writing in those days. (I knew about Virginia Woolf, of course, but she was childless and she had had money as well as Leonard, who so thoroughly supported her in other ways.)

When Bob Amussen wrote his first letter to me I replied in a very flippant manner, ending with the phrase which has, I suppose, come back to haunt me: "Literature is no substitute for life, except in extreme cases." However, I did, in the end, sign the contract with Bobbs-Merrill. (Edward Weeks was very gracious, and wrote to Bob saying that I wrote with "fire in my pen." How was I ever going to live up to any of this?)

Once we had returned home I worked to finish the book of stories and began to think about the novel. The book of stories, *Ten Green Bottles* (now out of print), came out in August 1967, and we had another little girl in November. I felt, once again, that much as I loved writing, I loved my family more — got more pleasure from them, felt more fulfilled. I had to shut the world out while doing the actual work of writing, and I wasn't convinced that that was a good thing. So I made a vow that November: I would never write when the children were around. I would never say "Shh, go away. I'm writing." But I *would* write.

It might take me longer to finish things, but that didn't matter. I wanted it *all* and this was my solution. I still think it was a good one. Talent really isn't enough; discipline has to be there as well. I'm not talking about genius — I'm quite interested in genius and spontaneity, lack of discipline, "divine disorder," etc., but that's not my subject here. The demands of a young family simply forced discipline upon me. If I didn't use the time when the older two were at school and the baby was asleep, then tough luck — that was all the time there was. I'm not really a very organized person by nature, so for me, these constraints were a good thing. You may be thinking, "But didn't you ever feel frustrated, your mind crammed with grocery lists, doctor's appointments, PTA meetings, cookies to bake, clothes to mend, stories to listen to and read — all the *stuff* that the homemaker (usually a woman) has to deal with?" I can honestly say no — no I didn't. I did whine about not having a room or even a corner of a room of my own. We'd had a big mahogany desk made for me in West Africa, and had brought it back with us. But it sat in one corner of the dining-room and was used as a kind of sideboard and catch-all, covered in caps and mittens, games, projects, bills to pay. I wrote at the kitchen table, cleared up before 2:30 (it all went into a cardboard box), and wrote again that night when all was still.

I finished the first draft of *Songs My Mother Taught Me* some time in 1968 I think — I can't remember exactly when, and sent it off to Bobbs-Merrill. (I think I paid Bill Schermbrucker to type it or we made some kind of barter arrangement; he was living in our upstairs suite in those days.) They didn't like it: the reader didn't like it; Bob Amussen didn't like it. So much for Katherine Mansfield and the early James Joyce; so much for fire in the pen. At this point the manuscript ended when Harry, forced into selling his beloved "camp" in the mountains, decides to burn it down instead. Isobel watches from her hiding place in one of the old hollowed-out tree trunks which border one side of the property. I can't remember how I got rid of the rest of the family — and the housekeeper — for the day, and I no longer have that manuscript. Perhaps I sent them on a picnic. I know I didn't want any loss of life, but I did want a big fire, a Wagnerian ending. "Think again," said my editor.

I put the novel, the *failure*, in a drawer. I didn't forget about it, but I couldn't quite see how to fix it. I certainly felt under an obligation to write a novel but maybe this wasn't the novel I was meant to write. Life went on; life got pretty hectic. I remember this time as very happy. And in the back of my mind, at the back of the stove, as it were, a completely different novel was simmering.

I decided to apply for a writer's grant — I think back then they were four thousand dollars, plus travel. I had discussed with Ian the possibility of taking the kids and going to someplace warm and sunny, with cheap domestic help. I now knew what I really wanted to write about and I asked for some time off from my family duties if I got the grant. Vancouver was getting to me: we had a party line so I couldn't leave the phone off the hook; I was rude to the poor woman who called and asked me to contribute to the Bunny Bus. I was even ruder to a woman who wanted to remind Ian he was teaching a painting workshop on Saturday. I told her to call back — I wasn't taking messages. (She'd asked if I had a pencil handy. Later she said to Ian "Do you live in a boarding-house?" She thought I was the grumpy landlady!) I was learning that if you "worked" at home you weren't really working; *real* work meant going out to work.

I decided we would go to Portugal, perhaps to the Algarve, if I got the grant. Ian wouldn't be able to come; he was teaching at UBC and was too new to ask for a leave. But the rest of us would go for six months and he would come over at Christmas.

I got the grant and we immediately began to have second thoughts. I wasn't at all worried about travelling with the kids: the older two had already proved themselves to be excellent travellers and the baby was happy to be wherever there were familiar faces. But what if someone became ill? What if "cheap domestic help" turned out to be a cheap romantic dream? What if the kids *didn't* like it? I could see the logic in all of this (some of these questions even originated with me), but I was reluctant to give up the idea of getting away from Vancouver for a while, away from the telephone, the appliances — such as the fridge, which seemed to shout, "Clean me! Defrost me!" as I sat writing at the kitchen table. Just for a few months, I wanted sunlight and salads and three little blonde heads (supervised by my faithful Esmerelda) playing on the beach while I wrote.

I let go of this dream with great reluctance and gradually substituted another. My grandfather — the model, up to a point, for Harry in *Songs* — had died and left me part of a house in New York State. House prices were very depressed in that area; Binghamton is one of the many towns and small cities in the northeastern U.S. which had depended on localized light industry, and was then more or less fading away. SUNY keeps it going now. When the house was sold, I received about $6,000. U.S., and fearful that it would just disappear into the housekeeping, we had put a down-payment on a house just two blocks away and were renting it out. Now I suggested we sell that house and find and buy a small house or cottage in the country, or maybe on one of the Gulf Islands, to use as a retreat. I could go there for six months with the children and we'd see each other, be reunited as a family, every weekend.

In the end we found the place on Galiano Island. Ian, with help from Bill, worked like crazy to fix up the old abandoned house on the property. We all spent August there, and in September Ian and the two older girls returned to the city, while the baby (nearly two by then) and I waved them good-bye. I turned in my travel grant, paid for a housecleaner to come once a week, and promised everybody I would be Supermother on the weekends. It felt very strange, watching them drive off, and I wondered if I had done the right thing. Would I last a week? A day? How would Sarah and Vickie feel? How Ian?

A neighbour just down the path and across the road minded Claire five hours a day on weekdays — she had a boy Claire's age and a girl a year older. The book that was going to take me six months (at least) to finish was finished just before my birthday in mid-November. I was writing like mad, page after page after page, and in a strange, discontinuous style — a kind of collage, a kind of poem. (This book was *Mrs. Blood*.) At the end of

November we went home, where I sprained my ankle badly tripping over our idiot dog, and we didn't come back until the end of February, when once again Claire and I remained alone during the week. I made some revisions — not many — and wrote yet another novel, a short one, *Munchmeyer & Prospero on the Island*, just for fun. I was filled with joy, giddy with it: I *was* a writer, not a one-book-wonder. Bob Amussen came out for a visit and loved *Mrs. Blood*. It was published in New York in 1970, and was eventually published by Talonbooks as well. On the first of May, Ian came out to get Claire and me, the dog and the cat, and we all went home. We had fallen in love with our ramshackle place on Galiano by this time, and realized it could be everybody's retreat, not just mine.

What I found on Galiano was not just peace but what I suppose you could call my "style." I do not — in my novels at least — write a continuous narrative. My mind simply doesn't work that way and I'm not comfortable with that structure. When I took up *Songs* again, in 1972, I knew how I wanted to structure it. Chronologically, yes, but with things jumping in: rhymes, children's games, the detritus of childhood that most of us carry with us. I also — just as I had done with *Mrs. Blood* — wanted to set up a tension in the narrative by telling more than one story. I did that in the *Songs* manuscript by deciding to include a second part to Isobel's story — her work at the mental hospital, "the Hill." Now, she finally gets a certain amount of distance from her family, realizes how crazy and sad they really are, and that she is going to have to leave if she doesn't want to be destroyed by their anger and despair. This time I felt the novel "worked."

It's a long time ago, now, since I found a way to finish *Songs My Mother Taught Me*, and much has happened in the world, in my life, since then. I can now see "clumsinesses" in the book, but have decided to let them be. This book is, after all, part of my writing history. I *still* think literature is no substitute for life. And I still write on the kitchen table.

Galiano Island
May 1993

to Ian, Sarah, Victoria, Claire and Kathleen
and the summer of '72

All things fall and are built again
And those that build them again are gay

Songs
of
Innocence

Harry took Jane on one knee, Isobel on the other. "Listen," he said, "I'll teach you a little story."
"The night was dark and stormy
the rain came down in
torrents
The king said unto Antonio, 'Antonio, tell us a tale.'
Antonio began as follows:
'The night was dark and
stormy
The rain came down in
torrents'
The king said unto Antonio, 'Antonio, tell us a tale.'
Antonio began as follows ...."

one

Rome. Syracuse. Ithaca. Troy. Years later I was to wonder what scholar-gypsy had wandered through our state, bestowing such illustrious names on places (which seemed to me then, years later) so singularly lacking in lustre. Vestal. Ninevah. Oxford. Delhi. Cincinnatus.

But then, aged five and chair tilted dangerously as I leaned, kneeling, across the dining-room table to better see the map (a new one each year, free of charge at the Esso Dealer and as crisp and glamorous as the ten-dollar bills we got from Harry each birthday and each Christmas), I would trace with sure but excited fingers the arteries and veins of the vast complex of New York, following the route of the family's visits with something, perhaps, of the spirit of that unknown man or men who had seen fit to scatter the names, if not the seeds, of antiquity amongst prosaic towns named after more recent and trans-atlantic glories.

"Watch her, Warren," said my mother, "She'll fall!"

At first I knew only enough to put my finger on Utica. "That's where we'll stop for lunch." Utica was one of the first words I could spell, and "U" was, for a long, long while a magic letter.

"U"

> Dear Harry,
> How are U?
> Love,
> Isobel

"Warne! Watch her, she'll fall!" So that here too I made a mistake and thought his name was WARN WARN and not Warren J. Cleary, named proudly by his mother long before she dried up and shrivelled and was twisted into the deaf and half-dead old lady who lived in a wheelchair next door and spent her days looking out of the upstairs back-bedroom window at the two blue spruce her son, named after General Joseph Warren and the battle of Bunker Hill, had planted thirty-five years before. Had she ever been a girl named Sharon and had she ever worn the gay hat with the partridge feather as she did in the little silver picture frame on the top of our old piano?

The dining room table was real maple, second hand, and had a sanded-down place at one corner where Mother had removed somebody else's initials. There were white rings from hot coffee cups, and we stuck our chewing gum underneath the edge. The map was spread out flat so that I could look at it.

It seemed so close — Daddy could touch where we were, right now, with his thumb and then touch Utica without really moving his third finger. So that at first, aged three and four and five, I would fidget and sigh and feel an enormous sense of betrayal as the old car went on and on through farmland and dairyland, through towns with shuttered houses the colour of blackboard chalks — pale and dusty in the hot afternoon — while our father lit up yet another Lucky Strike and our mother said,

"Mind you don't throw that out the window. It'll come back in on the girls."

The dog's ears blew straight back from her head and her tongue hung out like a piece of delicatessen ham.

"Is it yet, Daddy?"

"Not yet."

"Is it yet?"

"Not yet."

"I'm hungry."

Until hypnotized by the heat and motion of the car, I fell asleep. Jane sat quietly next to me eating a package of Necco wafers she hadn't wanted to share. Or undressing her doll and dressing it up again.

Until gradually, with the accumulation of remembered summers, I grew to understand the relativity of the map and how, really, Utica was only the starting place. When we reached Utica we still had fifty miles to go, but once outside the landscape changed and we had a sense of "nearly there." The minute blue tear-shaped lake, which I projected from time to time on the roof of the car, moved closer now, was growing bigger, reaching out to us. We sighed, with the general relief of voyagers who have passed the worst of their hardships and perils. Entered a long avenue of pines.

"There," said our mother (as she always did), "you can smell the mountains now."

Heads out the window as far as we dared (and despite our mother's dire warnings about another car coming along and beheading us), we would strain into the dusk, inhaling the sharp piney smell (which meant Harry, which meant liberty) and take bets on who would be the first to see the lake. We shivered as we moved past brush-covered ditches where robbers from Canada hid.

But really too dark to see anything except the occasional winking lights of a cottage through the trees. Past the exhausted, weather-beaten houses of the year-round people, whom we envied with all our hearts. Past the fires from the public campsite. Past Red's Baits, where our father always slowed down; then, forestalled by his wife's "For heaven's sake, Warren, it's already past their bedtime!" and his own recollection of how much unpacking would have to be done before he could sit out on the front porch and smoke a quiet cigarette, he would speed up again through the village (general store and sub-post office, Adams' Dance Hall, a small bakery) — again the desire to stop and talk, to incorporate himself into the landscape of summer, "Anything we need?", again thwarted by the stinging flick of his wife's tongue. Finally the turn-off and the brief, uncomfortable bumping along the sandy road which led to the cottage. He shifted into low to take the hill, and the headlights caught the sign hanging there by the side of the road: JOURNEY'S END and, underneath, PRIVATE PROPERTY: TRESPASSERS WILL BE PROSECUTED. When I was old enough to really read, rather than to know the letters and words by habit, I came to associate these trespassers with those in the Lord's Prayer. I saw them coming in the wintertime, strange, tattered, desperate creatures, some barefoot in the snow, some holding children in their arms. Trying the locks of the deserted cottage. Breathing against the frosted windowpanes. All sinful. All to be forgiven. Except by Harry (Trespassers Will Be Prosecuted) and therefore why by me?

But now we had passed the sign and could see the lights of the cottage. The cool, fragrant smell of the night was almost unbearable and when our father turned the engine off the peepers, startled into silence for a moment, began again to saw away at the dark.

Our grandfather would descend the steps with a kerosene lantern, and for a minute, because we were sleepy and hungry and intoxicated by our first contact with the mountains in nearly a year, we would stare appalled at this sinister, fire-faced creature, lit from below — all dark hollows around the mouth and eyes — and his equally sinister upraised hand, the golden hairs picked out like some pale and ominous fur. Then "Grandpa" we would cry and struggle to get the door handle free (it had been tied up with string and the string caught in the window after dark). Our father would laugh nervously and roll down the window, releasing us to tumble out, legs unsteady, into the vast wool-scratchy embrace of our grandfather.

"Here. What's the matter with you two? You'll catch the whole damn place on fire." And he would scoop us up, leaving the lantern on the bottom step, carrying us squealing and kicking up to the top, where the three of us, Harry, Jane and Isobel, would stand looking down in arrogant superiority at the superfluous couple below. Our father began untying stuff from the top of the car.

"What'd you bring this time?" called our grandfather. "Fort Knox?"

We opened the screen door and went inside, where the housekeeper was heating up milk for cocoa and a plate of cookies had already been set out.

Even in our fatigue we looked around anxiously to see if anything had changed. Would we be given our own enamelled mugs — mine blue, my sister's green? Would the cookies be on one of the rainbow-rimmed "special" dinner plates? They would. We were.

We sat on the buffalo rug in front of the fire. Somewhere far away the dog had already challenged a raccoon.

"Hello, brats," said Harry, sitting down in "his" chair by the old radio.

"Hello." We sipped at our cocoa and looked at one another. The new housekeeper had put a marshmallow on top. She'd do.

There was a time, before my time, when Journey's End did not exist. But that was like knowing that once the earth had not existed — possible but incomprehensible. I knew only that every summer, for as far back as I could remember, we had packed up, left notes for the milkman and the paper boy, made some arrangement with whatever neighbour we were speaking to that year and gone to spend the summer in the mountains. There *had* been changes in our lives: We had moved house three times, once to go and live in Ithaca for a year while our father got a Master's Degree and we dined off three-legged turkeys and blue-shelled eggs bought cheap from the experimental poultry farm; we had both started school; our grandmother Goodenough had died — and that's when Grandpa started asking us to call him "Harry" or "Uncle Harry." If we forgot, in public, he'd laugh and say, "Now what did I tell you about that?" Yet we always spent our summers in the mountains. First there was no electricity and no running water — a red-handled pump halfway down the forest path to the beach below, a pump that had to be primed with a mug of water saved from the day before. A green-painted outhouse that smelled of carbolic, a scary place that could suck you down, if you weren't careful, into the unspeakable dark below the seat. (Or enamel potty pails, with lids, kept in each bedroom for use at night. Terribly cold to sit on in the dark, and your pee coming out so loud that the hired man, who often slept over in the next room, might hear you and laugh at your weakness. But better than a torch and the dark inside the outhouse late at night.) Beautiful old hurricane lamps — we were allowed to clean the chimneys, very carefully, with a paper towel. A tin candlestick of my own with a picture of Jack-Be-Nimble. Later a pump, a generator, even (much later), a telephone. The *blackness* when a candle was blown out. The smell of kerosene. The light from the radio dial. Figures coming and going — dissolving, re-creating themselves, in front of the huge stone fireplace. A shadow-mother on the bedroom wall.

After we got electricity there was a curious rectangular clock on the mantelpiece. It had three square-faceted wheels that click, click, clicked in place and gave the hour, the minute, the second. But not the year or the day, so that it might seem, if one didn't glance at the Varga calendar on the kitchen wall, that the summers at Journey's End were all part of one minutely recorded but immortal and circular day. Or if one ignored the faint pencil marks by the back door where Harry measured us each year. Even at ten, however, I knew better. Would sit on the buffalo rug in front of the fire, squinting up at the clock, my fingers on my wrist.

8:01
8:02

Counting to myself, "Seventy-nine, eighty, eighty-one."

8:03

and whispering inside my head, "Isobel, you are dying faster than the day."
("Isobel! What are you doing there? Get up and go to bed.")
9:00

But Harry was no primitive, and the cottage, more lodge than cottage, was constantly being improved. Down in his workshop underneath the cottage he had shelves forced into the damp orange sand, and on these shelves were tobacco tins full of nails of all sizes, jars of paintbrushes, tins of paint, boards stacked against the wall. I was heady from the smell of turps and wood-shavings, stuck my face into old paint rags. Aah. He had built the whole place himself, with some local help — a large rectangular structure sloping away from the hill overlooking the lake so that the rear of the house was ten feet off the ground, leaving room for his workshop on one side, an underground garage on the other. Half-logs were used, smooth on the inside of the house, curved on the outside. Left with their bark still on to blend with the forest and the lake. He cleared only where he had to. The trees were all around us.

On one side of the cottage there were many charred stumps among the second growth — the result of a fire over half a century before. We used to play in these stumps, some of which were no more than shells of full pine cones and pine needles. Made tiny eye-holes and stared at our elders, coming and going — near enough to be touched but never found. Once I hid two rag dolls, mother and baby, whom I called "Me" and "Mimi," in one of these stumps (I think we were kidnappers that day) and couldn't find them again. We looked and looked, but it was hopeless. Ten years later I came upon them by accident, bleached featureless by the wind and sun and rain — the big doll's leg chewed ragged by some forest creature. It was like finding two small corpses; I left them there, covered them up with pine needles and went away. For all I know they are still there in the forest. Isobel, perhaps they are your totems?

We slept at one end of the house, near the woodpile and next to the hired man's room; Harry slept at the other, the room that was to become the bathroom between him and the house-keeper's room. Our mother thought it wasn't decent and the housekeeper should have the hired man's room, but Harry just laughed and said "nonsense."

We actually had two rooms, separated only by a faded, flow-ered curtain. My mother slept in a bed, my father on an army cot. My sister and I slept in a big double bed in the other room, a room obviously intended originally for them. There was a door that shut all this out from the big main room, and on this door

Harry had taped up a printed diagram of a human body, showing all the veins and arteries (in black and blue) and the major pressure points. The head was turned sideways, and the background colour was orange-red, like blood. I hated this poster, particularly as it was on "our" door. Now I wonder if it wasn't another of Harry's practical jokes. He was very contemptuous of my father and may have known how he felt about blood and death. Still, it stayed there for seventeen years and no one ever had a major accident, so it may have served a purpose after all.

Once the door was closed and the candle blown out or the lights turned off, the four of us were left alone with our thoughts and our dreams and one another. Jane and I, in our oatmeal-coloured Doctor Dentons, curled up with each other and tried to be asleep before our parents came in. Sometimes we could hear the sharp "slap" of a beaver's tail down below us in the creek, sometimes the manic laughter of a loon. Always the frogs and peepers, the little chipmunks hurrying along the roof. But if my parents weren't quarrelling they were snoring heavily and then it was very hard to get to sleep. Anything could set my mother off — the way the housekeeper handed her the biscuits, the way my father "kowtowed" to his father-in-law, the fact that it was all very well for us to come up here and freeload every summer but where did that leave her? The fact that she did all the dirty work while he went out and sat on his backside in a rowing boat.

My father would mutter. NNah. NNah. NNah. A ducklike sound. Sometimes she called him "Donald Duck," and we, our mother's daughters, giggled into our pillows. Or sometimes she would start to cry and say we couldn't come here any more and then our blood ran cold. "If it weren't for the children I wouldn't come here at all. What's in it for me? Did you see the way he gets her to buy the meat? Giggling and carrying on like a schoolgirl and they all know she's his housekeeper. You're a queer bunch, all of you. Why should I put up with it?"

This was usually worse on Saturday nights after we had made our weekly trip to Excelsior, where Harry did the shopping, farmed out the dirty laundry to a local woman, changed books and jigsaw puzzles at the lending library. Our father always found some excuse to go too ("Better get this here back tire checked") and our mother "went along for the ride." We opted to go in the LaSalle with our grandfather and the housekeeper. Out past the sign — *Journey's End* — down the sandy road past milkweed, black-eyed Susans, blueberry bushes still full, as if by magic, in spite of all our picking. Turn right at the mailboxes and onto the paved road. Past the Trinity Fish and Game Club, the Volunteer Fire Department, then left this time onto the main road to Lake Constance and Excelsior and the excitement mounting. Harry drove fast but not recklessly, a Panama hat pushed to the back of his head and his sunburned hands curled loosely around the wheel. Past the inn with its elaborate golf course and gay-shirted figures shimmering in the heat as they moved slowly across the manicured lawns. These were the people from New York, or farther, up for a week or two, "foreigners" in our eyes. Our mother suspected this inn because it had a cocktail bar and an Austrian proprietor. Once, just after the war, we convinced ourselves that we saw Adolf Hitler peer from behind net curtains at an upstairs window. We were sure the innkeeper harboured German spies. Past the Y.M.C.A. camp with its faded blue triangle, the camp itself hidden way back in the trees although sometimes the boys were seen, tee-shirted and laughing, coming back in an untidy line from a hike. Or the director's station wagon full of tall sunburned young men heading into town.

The "Log Cabin" new and as yet unassimilated, somehow too rustic with its glimpse of checked tablecloths and copper candlesticks seen through the windows. We knew this journey the way we knew the exact location of the furniture in the cottage. Could shut our eyes at any stage along the way and then say, "Now!" And the Fire Department, the inn, the boys' camp, would spring up, predictably, as we opened them. The journey to town, like the journey to the woods, was almost a religious experience, with us children as novitiates recognizing and genuflecting before the necessary stations of our ecstasy. Except that the journey to Excelsior was less intense because more frequent, more familiar. Nor did it begin any experience so large and important as a summer.

Nevertheless we loved the trip — loved the feeling of the whole thing, almost Sabbath, as we sat, freshly braided, in clean pinafore dresses and wearing shoes, watching the afternoon unroll before us from the window of Harry's car. When we arrived, laughing because the Buick was still a small, insignificant green speck way down the road, we would climb the steep (at first) steps to the wooden boardwalk and follow Harry and the housekeeper into the grocery and general store. Everyone greeted him: "Afternoon, Mr. Goodenough." "Afternoon." We basked in the general glory of being with him, of being almost attached to him, a child on each side. The housekeeper passed him the list and he strode down the narrow aisles, selecting canned goods, a crate of oranges, great sensuous watermelons with lacquered seeds, a bushel basket of corn. He was always waited on by the proprietor himself, a man whose bleached hair and leathery face showed customers that although he kept a store he didn't hang about in it all day and all night every day, no sir. Harry would point to something and the proprietor would jerk his head in the direction of one of the eternal pimply-faced boys who were "helping out" for the summer.

"You there, Fred" (or Jim or Leroy), "get Mr. Goodenough a case of Campbell's pork 'n beans." The very breadth of Harry's shopping never ceased to delight us, although the storekeeper acted as though it were perfectly natural to order food by the case, Chinet plates by the gross, six dozen oranges and a five-gallon tin of maple syrup. And when Harry came to pay we would stare incredulously at the roll of bills in his hand, never quite believing it wasn't play money or that the storekeeper wouldn't suddenly turn and say with a nasty smile, "You'll have to put it all back yourself, you know," as had happened to us once back home when our father was refused any more credit at Conklin's Grocery Store.

There would be an uneasy moment when the money changed hands, and sometimes I wandered away at this point, too tense and excited to stand still. But nothing ever had to be put back, and Harry would pocket the change without counting it, chatting for a few minutes with the proprietor's wife.

"These aren't your little granddaughters, are they?"

"All mine, I'm afraid."

"Would you ever! My, haven't they grown since last summer."

And Harry would glare at us from under the brim of his Panama hat. "You two brats. C'm here. Have you been growing while I wasn't looking?"

Giggling. "Yes, Grandpa."

"What'd I tell you about that?"

"Yes, Harry."

"That's better. Well, I guess you'd better have some candy to stunt your growth."

And he would take out the change again while the proprietor's wife reached for two Hershey bars and said, "No, no, Mr. Goodenough. This is my treat."

Daddy and Mother usually went to the hardware store first or to the small, untidy summer library where there seemed to be cats, like motorized bookends, everywhere asleep on the shelves. But what my father really liked to do was to wander into the grocery store, casually, his hands in the pockets of his summer trousers.

"Afternoon."

"Afternoon."

And if a new boy came to wait on him he'd say, quickly, "Naw. It's all right. I'm with m' father-in-law," then move over to us and slap our backsides. "Well, kids, havin' a good time?" And we would smile uneasily at him, ashamed for and of him with his phony country-boy accent, his hands in his pockets and nothing to buy. I felt deeply my father's equivocal position, although when I was alone with Jane and Harry and the housekeeper I never felt my own. Now I wished he would go away, would not have to endure the spectacle of Harry buying, as he well knew, for his wife, himself, his children. Sometimes his father-in-law would grin at him over his shoulder.

"What took you so long — flat tire?"

"Naw," he would mumble. "That old Buick's not very good

now. I have to take her careful." Harry would nod and wink at us, then turn back to his list.

Sometimes our father would go to the counter with us, ostensibly to buy some cigarettes, really to initiate talk.

"Well, what d'ya think of the kids, eh? Ain't they grown?" Or "What would you like, kids" A Babe Ruth? A Mars bar? Guess I'll take three Mars Bars and a package of Luckies, thanks." Then he would hand over the money with a flourish, and we would mumble our thank-yous and escape into the hot, dusty air. Our father ran his hand wistfully along the axe handles as he went out.

Yet he was afraid of sharp things, let Harry and the hired man chop the firewood, cautioned me over and over again not to run with a lollipop in my mouth, scissors in my hand, the ice pick, the bread knife, the kitchen cleaver.

"Isobel! Put that damn thing down before you answer the telephone." Flinching and moving sideways as though I had already nicked him.

Hated Harry's old-fashioned straight-edged razor. Was afraid of life.

We bought our meat across the way, up another flight of steps and three along. For one whole summer of the war only the housekeeper, a still-young Southern woman with a soft lazy voice and a passion for revival meetings and sweet-potato pie, went in all alone. Harry laughed at the way she could get thick chops or the best cuts of meat without using any stamps. Jane and I would wander up and down outside, for we hated the sticky, fishy smell of the place and the constant flies. We could see Mae-Love through the dusty glass, laughing at something the butcher said, her plump elbows, white and creamy as best lard, resting on the counter, her head thrown back. Then she would come out with an armful of paper-wrapped parcels, the blood already beginning to seep through, and we quickly got into the car, which Harry had driven up and parked just outside. Harry put the meat in a wooden box full of ice wrapped in old newspapers, threw a rug over it and we all got in to drive up a side road and deliver the laundry. Mae-Love (who wouldn't let us call her Mrs. Woolcock) told Harry that butcher was a "real caution" and Harry laughed a different sort of laugh than his usual sort.

Or sometimes we would go from the grocery store to the post office next door to read the Wanted posters. For years there was a black man, Floyd Masters, gradually fading away on the post office wall. I remember him because he was black and because he was said to have "maroon eyes." ("How much reward d'you think?" "Not much. It doesn't say he killed a man." We searched everywhere.) Then switched allegiances and waited for our parents because Harry usually went straight back home after delivering the laundry but Daddy continued on through Excelsior and out to the Point where there was a combined drugstore/souvenir shop and soda fountain and where red-faced men in Hawaiian shirts were ranged along the front porch talking trout and drinking Spur or Coca-Cola in thirsty fish-mouthed gulps. Mr. Reynolds, who ran the store, had incredibly smooth, hairless skin, as though his outer surface had been peeled off. He was a Mason. My father, his eyes still dazed by the sun, would hesitate, hand on the screen door, searching out Mr. Reynolds from among the shelves of Skol and Pepsodent, Sloan's Liniment, Absorbine Junior, razor blades and cheap cologne. For a minute he would stand there, uncertain, his brow puckered, while Mother and Jane and I waited impatiently in line behind him.

"Go on, for heaven's sake. You're letting all the flies in!" Mother would give him a little shove with the flat of her hand. The loafers on the porch looked up and grinned at one another.

"Come *on*, Daddy. It's hot out here!" Then he would find what he was searching for and advance, swaggering a little.

"Brother Reynolds!"

Mr. Reynolds, after a quick frown, trying to remember who...

"Brother — Ah. How are you, Brother?" They clasped hands and exchanged the secret, mystical sign.

"Brother Warren Cleary. Three Forks Blue Lodge. H.B. Goodenough's son-in-law. Over at Trinity."

"That's right. I remember you all right. How are you?"

Smiling at us. "How's the family?" My mother thawed, but only slightly.

"We're quite well, thank you. How are your wife and children?" She hated the Masons, called it "kid stuff" for "mama's boys and perverts," but Mr. Reynolds had a nice smile and his wife, poor thing, had to live up here summer and winter, even though they had enough to go to Florida. He was a regular skinflint, in spite of his nice smile.

Daddy steered us toward the soda fountain.

"What'll you have, kids? Treat's on me. C'mon, Clara. What'll you have?" He sat down on one of the red stools and motioned us to follow.

"Just a small Dixie cup, thank you, Mr. Reynolds. Lemon sherbet if you've got it. Or pineapple. I don't like anything rich."

"One lemon sherbet, we've got it. What about you girls?" His smooth pale skin and white druggist's jacket seemed appropriate to the glass and chrome. He looked so clean — incredibly antiseptic.

I always chose a sarsaparilla soda because I liked the sound of it. And Jane and Daddy usually had chocolate sundaes. I ate my ice cream first and then sucked at the cool brown liquid, slowly, trying not to make noises with my straw. Jane marbled her sundae with a spoon.

"Don't do that!" Mother licked at her wooden spoon with small catlike motions of her tongue.

"Why not?"

"It's bad manners, that's why not. Eat like a lady or you can't come out with us."

Jane looked at her blankly, then nodded once and returned to her sundae. Mr. Reynolds left to sell some sunglasses and then came back.

"How's the fishing?"

"Oh. Not so good, you know. Better on this lake, I guess, than ours. I've been mostly goin' after brook trout this summer."

"Wait another couple of years and those fish you put in will taste real nice on a cold morning."

"You betcha. You can't catch 'em now, but some fellow at Higgin's Bay caught a thirty-two pounder last week. Wonder where he'd been hidin'."

"Oh. They're crafty all right. Real crafty."

Mother had finished her Dixie cup.

"Warne, don't you think it's time to be getting along?"

"Yeah. Yeah. Sure. Hang on a minute, can't you?" "Here," he would say, giving us each a quarter, "see what you can buy with this."

We slid off our stools and went to the back room where the souvenir items were kept: sateen pillows stuffed with pine needles, "Call of the Wild," "Sweet Dreams, Excelsior, New York," "Souvenir of Lincoln County," tee shirts ("Excelsior, N.Y." below an Indian head or a pine tree). Felt pennants. Incense burners in the shape of a little log cabins with a metal chimney where you put in the fragrant cones. Leatherette photo albums ("Our Holiday"). Billfolds, keyholders, moccasins decorated with beadwork — anything and everything proclaiming that you had been to the mountains for the summer. I really wanted a pillow, had always wanted one, but they cost a dollar. Finally I chose five postcards: a racoon by the water's edge, a doe and her fawn, two views of Trinity Lake and a card of an enormously fat woman in a pink-flowered bathing suit with the caption underneath "You catch the big'uns up here."

Mr. Reynolds, deep in conversation with my father, a fact I had counted on, took my quarter without looking through the cards.

"Found what you wanted, did you?"

"There's five."

"That's all right then. Five cents each. Thank you very much, young lady. Won't be very long until she *is*, eh?" He winked at my father.

"Yeah. Yeah." Awkwardly he put his arm around me. I could smell his sweat and moved away. Outside, my mother began to blow on the horn. Jane appeared from the comic book rack and we headed toward the door.

"See you soon, Brother Cleary."

"Yeah. Well, we'll probably be in every Saturday to do the shoppin'." He waved as we drove off.

"What do you want to make a fool of yourself in front of him for? And a fool of me." Our father was intent on his driving.

"What d'ya mean? Nobody made a fool of himself."

"That's your story! What do you think it looks like when you leave me hanging around in that place while you show off to some two-bit country drugstore operator who has to be nice to you because you give him the old Masonic glad-hand and corner him so he can't get away. Well, you can come by yourself next time. I don't want your Dixie cups and your rotten manners."

And so it would continue, in the evening, after our usual late Saturday dinner of fried chicken, biscuits, corn and sweet-potato pie.

"Would you mind passing up that corn, Mr. Goodenough? Sure is good."

"What d'you want to make a pig of yourself? It's not as though you're paying for any of it, is it?"

"NNah. NNah. NNnah."

I had addressed all the postcards to myself.

> "Dear Isobel.
>   Having a swell time.
>   Your friend.
>   I"

and put them under my pillow. Jane had saved her quarter. She was going to buy seeds and win a Columbia bike or some ballbearing roller skates. Eventually both our parents fell asleep. Soon they were snoring and all was quiet except the night sounds of the creatures inside and out and the far-off sound of a fiddle from the Fish and Game Club dance. The sound went on and on, very faint, beneath the benevolent postcard moon.

I fell asleep and dreamed of a man with maroon eyes who would carry me off to a dance and we would eat watermelon side by side, having a contest to see who could spit the pips the far-thest, laughing as the dancers slipped and slid in wild confusion.

Then fell deeper into sleep, to the very bottom of the well where there is only peace and darkness.

And was still.

two

But who was Isobel when she was awake? Daughter of Warren Joseph Cleary, and Clara Blake, née Goodenough, Cleary, younger sister of Jane Elizabeth, who walks beside her, black-gowned and white surpliced in the Junior Choir.

> Love divine
> All Love Ex-cell-ell-ing

Joy
of Heav'n
   to Ear-rth
      Come Down.

Who believed in hell and damnation. Who had killed her grandmother and longed to kill her mother and possibly her pa.

> Fixed in Uh-us Thy Humble
> Dwell-ell-ing

The choir master had a wooden leg and took me on his knee.

"Isobel why do you look so sad?"

"I'm thinking about my grandma."

Who won a Holy Bible with Helps for memorizing 101 selected verses from the Testaments Old and New.

Who inhabited a world where outside in the streets waited a veritable Halloween of robbers, rapists, rabid dogs and cats who could scratch your eyes out; rusty tin can lids and jagged, hidden shards of glass; accidents, treacheries and betrayals.

Who would sometimes in the night wake from a dream to hear the ambulances, wild with hunger, prowling the city streets, looking for her, for me.

"Mother!"

"What is it now?" Puffy with sleep at the bedroom door.

"I'm frightened!"

"Don't be silly, Isobel. Go back to sleep."

"Isobel is such a high-strung child," my mother said to the druggist. Then warned us again to be sure and look both ways.

("What is a stranger, Isobel?" asked Harry when I was six.

"Strangers are usually men.")

Who lived in a town of two rivers, the Tioga and the Owego but knew nothing whatsoever about the town except that which she was allowed to know.

"Isobel, where are you going?"

"Roller skating."

"Be careful. Go up on the grass if you can't stop at the bottom of the hill."

Who wore her skate key around her neck like the other kids but wasn't of them.

"Let's go down Bennett Hill. C'mon."

"Yes, let's."

"Are you coming Isobel?"

"No. I don't want to."

"You're scared."

"I'm not. I just don't want to come."

Watched them fly away like birds, their skirts feathering out behind them. And never fall.

"Isobel, why have you come back?"

"I didn't feel like skating any more."

Loved the story of the Ugly Duckling and looked in the mirror and waited.

Drying my hair in front of the oven's open door in winter, sitting on an orange crate between my mother's knees; she rubbed my head between the folds of towel. Talked always about the past and praised my crowning glory. Of Harry's four dead sisters who were beautiful and had hair the colour of straw, of gold, of copper — "Like you, Isobel" — of chestnuts in September — "Like you, Jane." I loved the feeling of the warm water pouring over my downcast head, the squeak of my clean hair, the long pull, pull of the hairbrush.

Jane, finished first, was sitting at the kitchen table in her bathrobe, dipping baker's chocolate into a saucerful of sugar.

But she washed it only once a month, in wintertime, and on our hygiene charts we put in lying, nervous √'s under WASHED HAIR every week.

Baths, too, were rationed in the winter, as there was no heat in either of the bathrooms.

Mother brought in an old electric heater with a cone-shaped element. It glowed behind a wire mesh circle like a catcher's mask.

Daddy stood uneasy at the doorway — we could be electrocuted at any minute.

"Watch out with that heater, Clara!"

And she, bitter, kneeling by the tub and scrubbing our backs with a soapy cloth.

"Would you rather they got pneumonia and we had another pile of doctor's bills?"

I trembled to think of my mother, in one of her sudden rages, picking up the heater and flinging it at us, helpless, in the bath. Screaming once, "Turn it off, turn it off, we don't need it!" and she, contemptuous, "Don't be silly."

Sometimes she did our hair up in rags or bread papers if there were a birthday party or a special assembly the next day at school. The lumps of hair dug into the back of our heads and we couldn't sleep. But usually we wore it braided tight against our temples, sometimes with plaid taffeta ribbons on the ends.

"You have lovely hair, Isobel, Jane. Don't you ever forget it."

Changing her mind, however, later on, as we grew older. Our hair's straightness cancelling out its colour. She gave us foul-smelling amateurish home permanents, jerking at our heads when the rods and end papers refused to wind up the way it promised in the diagram. Running out of the special pins so that the absorbent cotton turned purple, as did our ears and the backs of our necks.

"Sit still!"

"I'm tired, I want to go to bed!"

"Just a few more. I'm not doing this for my pleasure, I assure you." The burning smell of the lotion in my nose, the sticky feel of it running down my neck.

Heads wrapped in towels like victims of some identical brain surgery, we sat waiting for the alarm clock and staring dully at the clippings she had pasted on the bathroom wall.

> This is a Watchbird Watching a
> Mealie-Mouth
> This is a Watchbird Watching
> You
> Were you a Mealie-Mouth this Month?

The permanents smelled and usually came out within a week.

One Christmas she took us to André's for professional cold waves before we had our yearly studio portraits taken. We sat on extra cushions in the big black leatherette seats and had our hair done by Miss Anne and Miss Vera — after it had been styled first by André himself, a tall, thin European man in a mustard-coloured linen jacket. Miss Anne and Miss Vera wore pink rayon coveralls and rubber gloves when they applied the setting lotion.

"Are they going to be flower girls?" (Every curler perfectly in place.)

"Oh no, no." Mother gave her little embarrassed, defensive laugh. "It's just that they have their portraits taken for their grandpa every year and this time we decided to make it extra special." All around us heads were being washed, trimmed, shaped, tinted, bleached and permed in preparations for the coming holidays. The operators wore corsages of fake holly berries and gilded pine cones and there was a little musical Christmas tree that circled round and round by the cashier's desk.

My father came in for the third time, stamping his feet to see if we were ready.

"There. Aren't they lovely? Weren't they worth waiting for?"

Society women, waiting their turn in the anteroom, regarded us with eyes as cool as diamonds. I thought I looked terrible, just terrible, had been hoping for some miracle that would justify the torment of the permanent itself, the humiliation of hearing my mother relate our family history, in a confidential tone, to yet another set of polite but indifferent listeners. A beautiful teenager, probably waiting to have her hair done for the sorority ball, regarded my glossy curls with open amusement and I hurried into my galoshes and scarf "("You'd better bundle up, kids, it's snowin' to beat the band out there"), desperate to get out and away from the place. Mother gave the cashier something on account with a cheque she knew would bounce and, after we had rushed over to Macleod's and into our new Christmas dresses for the picture, we all went to the Home Dairy for dinner.

"Eat up, Isobel. You won't get anything else tonight."

And what did Jane think of all this, my sister, co-sharer of most of my sorrows? It was difficult to tell. Right now she was eating macaroni and cheese as though it was just another day, which perhaps, to her, it was. We talked sometimes, when the arguments were at their fiercest, of leaving home, of going to live with Harry. But we never told each other how we really felt or unveiled the dark abysses of our misery. Like strangers fleeing from a burning building, we turned aside to avoid seeing each other's nakedness. I can tell little of Jane; I never really knew her.

Of Isobel I knew a little more. From as far back as I could

remember I was aware — and afraid — of two things: death and the passage of time. ("Isobel, you are dying faster than the day.") On the way to the mountains each summer I tried to memorize each group of Burma Shave signs we passed, every new billboard or poster slapped against a barn. If someone made a remark and I didn't hear, I would be driven nearly frantic. "What did you say?" "Nothing." "No. You said something. What did you *say?*" "I can't remember now." "Please, oh please." And sometimes I would say to myself, "Ten years from now you will remember this moment and it will be the past." If something truly unusual happened I tried to impale the whole complex of sight/sound/touch/taste/smell on my consciousness and memory as though such an experience was like some rare and multicoloured butterfly. For example, one day when we stopped in Utica for a proper meal instead of the usual hamburger and milkshake, a group of midgets came and sat down at the table next to us. I thought they were grotesque and sad, with their high falsetto voices and aging skin. One of the little men had a blue polka dot bow tie and was smoking a big cigar. One of the tiny women was wearing a gardenia corsage; perhaps she was celebrating a birthday. Certainly they were very noisy. I immediately felt that the presence of these midgets, the *very first time* we had ever stopped to eat a sit-down meal in Utica, was of the utmost significance. Perhaps I was to give birth to a midget at some later date? A little thrill ran down my back. I shivered and began to try and memorize the afternoon: net curtains, tables covered with red-checked tablecloths, my father's cracked and dirty fingernails as he picked up a roll and buttered it, the hair that had started growing on my legs, the sunlight setting out a neat gold carpet by the door. I was eating macaroni salad, which I was mad about that year and had piled all the bits of green pepper (which I didn't like) in a little heap at one side of my plate. My mother told me to stop staring. "It isn't nice."

But I was so busy memorizing details that I neglected to leave myself open to listen, eavesdrop, overhear. I still wonder what those midgets were talking about and where they came from. Even as we left and I took a red-hot cinnamon toothpick from a dish by the cashier's desk I thought to myself, "You'll remember this all your life." Then we went out and got into the stuffy car (windows rolled up so the dog wouldn't try to jump out) and continued on our way, leaving the strange and vaguely sinister quartet still sitting over their strawberry shortcake and coffee. I knew they would not remember us at all. They would not remember me.

Another thought struck me suddenly and made me shiver. Even if we were to return to that restaurant a year from now and the midgets were still there laughing and joking and eating strawberry shortcake, I would have changed in size while they remained the same. They were locked into a relationship with tables, chairs, trees that seemed totally alien to my growing body. How could they bear it? How could they celebrate anything at all? How get up and dress and smile and go to bed? They were condemned to love one another, a separate race within a race, grotesques, freaks, creatures from one of my dreams. In a way I had not counted on I never forgot their faces.

It was the same with death. I was always conscious of it — that I or any of my family could die in our sleep or be struck down by madness or circumstance. Perhaps the two things go together: If you are aware of death you are aware of the passage of time; if you are aware of the passage of time you are aware of death. When my father had one of his asthma attacks I would lie in bed and listen to him coughing, coughing, coughing, gasping for breath and wheezing — would imagine him getting more and more red in the face until his heart would burst and he'd fall down dead in a pool of his own heart's blood. I fully expected it at any minute and secretly wished it so that the endless quarrels would indeed end and I could have some peace and wear a black band on the sleeve of my best winter overcoat. He himself was absolutely terrified of death, did not even want it mentioned. He attended Masonic funerals because he enjoyed the pomp and ceremony, but he sat near the back, I am sure. And once had a heart attack in the dentist's chair, no doubt out of fear that he wouldn't wake up from the gas.

("Is your mother home?"

"No, she's out shopping. Who is this?"

"I'm afraid there's been a little accident.")

Death was all around us and in some ways, like most children, we were attracted to it. We buried dead birds in juice tins or cigar boxes, dug them up again and again to see how they were getting on with the process of disintegration, were told — if caught at this — to wash our hands immediately because you never knew. Stamped on ants or crushed them between our fingers, gently but hard enough to kill, then buried them, with full honours — hymns, prayers and processions — in a special ant cemetery, one year, and even provided tombstones made from flat bits of rock.

> All things Bright and
> Beu-uu-tee-ful
> All Crea-tures
> Great
> A-and
> Small.

Our mother said we were "morbid" and told us again to wash our hands. The little boy up the street, who had blue lips and blue fingernails and wasn't allowed to run, died late one September night. Jerry La Face's father was electrocuted walking home from the golf course in a lightning storm. Somebody's mother had hanged herself in the shower. Suzanne Degnan was chopped up in Chicago and stuffed down a drain — her murderer was said to be definitely coming our way. The stairs creaked and alien beings stood in the night-black corners of my bedroom, tapped on my window to be let in, waited underneath the bed. We listened to *The Shadow* every Sunday night. He was brought to us by Blue Coal, and I could never convince myself that he wasn't somehow the arbiter of Wrong, not Right. "Who knows what evil lurks in the hearts of men?" Did he know I wished my parents were dead? Would he help me before I had a chance to take it back? "The Shadow Knows. Ha-ha-ha-ha-ha." "I don't know how you can listen to such tripe," said my mother. I looked at my sister Jane. *She* knew.

Twice a year we went to visit the family cemeteries to tidy up the graves and leave fresh plants. The Clearys were buried in Ross Park cemetery, out beyond the zoo, and my father would take clippers and a trowel and geraniums in terra-cotta-coloured cardboard pots which unhooked, like a shirt collar, to reveal a firm mass of roots and potting soil which he held in his left hand while he dug a little hole with his right. Then put the geranium in, his hands scented with damp earth and geranium leaves, and we would be sent to the public tap to fill up a mason jar with water.

When we went in June there were usually fresh flowers and plants everywhere, also little American flags, not yet faded, and the grass was green and soft. I didn't like to watch my father dig. In case he ... No. I must not think it. Would entice my sister away to look at tombstones while my mother sat in the car with a ladies' magazine, waiting. I remember a huge marble angel, very white as though he'd been cut out of sugar paper and pasted against the bright blue sky. He had a scroll in one hand and the other was raised up as though he were about to wave. Underneath it said "Whittaker" and there were lots of Whittakers lying in tidy rows in front. It always struck me how much the whole thing looked like a classroom. The angel was about to point at one of the Whittakers, perhaps John Jesse, 1843-1900, and he'd have to stand up and recite the Lord's Prayer or the Apostle's Creed all the way through before he could lie down again. Jane disagreed: "He looks like a traffic cop, not a teacher."

And the dead in there, underneath there, unable to see more than the angel's perfect marble toes and their collective surname on the pedestal. Unless they sat up. It was very pretty up where we were, with all the stones and grass and flowers: like a park, only quiet. But down there, just underneath, were all those people shut up in boxes and the worms were busy, busy, busy underneath our feet.

At Brownies we sang:

> Didja ever *think*
> When a hearse goes *by*

There's comin' a *time* when you're
Gon-na die?

There were never many people at the cemetery (we didn't go
on Memorial Day itself), and it was very peaceful to wander up
and down the rows. We liked to look at all the different stones,
grey, rose-coloured, white, even black. And some were small
and some were very big and fancy and had lots of carving on
them. That was when you were rich or important. Bankers or
owners of department stores or Jews.

Grandpa and Grandma Cleary were buried side by side, a
rose-coloured granite headstone replacing the old oak bedstead
(now my father's bed) where they'd lain together during their
married life. Joshua Warren Cleary, 1864-1933; Sharon
Elizabeth Cleary, 1870-1945, Wife of the Above. It was hard to
think of Grandma Cleary straightened out enough to lie flat
under one of those mounds, pressed like a flower underneath a
weight of earth. I always saw her, rather, on her back with her
legs twisted under her, her little hands, like bird's feet, hooked
and helpless above her breast. And it was hard to think of her as
Sharon the girl on the piano, with her young face and soft
brown hair and wonderful feathered hat.

There was room for Daddy and Mother too, although she
vowed she'd never be buried with a pack of Clearys. And room
for Aunt Olive and Uncle Pudge. But not Aunt Caroline,
because she was an RC and would have to be buried in St. Pat's.
My mother said she hoped when her time came somebody
would cremate her and throw her ashes away, wash them down
the kitchen sink, it was all the same to her. She didn't like the
Clearys when she was alive so why should she like them when
she was dead? My mother said terrible things and then changed
her mind and wanted you to forget them, but how could you?
Look how well Isobel remembers. Jane said she hated Mother,
but she didn't really meant it. I didn't say it because God might
hear me and I'd go to Hell.

Jane said your hair and fingernails kept on growing after you
were dead. They might grow right through the top of the coffin.

One day we walked quite a long way away from where my father was working.

"Look," said my sister, pointing.

"What?"

"There — that mausoleum."

"What about it?"

"Somebody's left the door open."

"Maybe they're inside."

We looked at each other, then back toward the Cleary grave and the car, but they were far away and hidden by a row of cypress trees.

"Let's go and see."

I was very frightened. When I was little I had thought the mausoleums were little churches where people came to pray for the dead. Then they had seemed charming. But now I knew. We approached cautiously. Some crazy paving led to the door, which was certainly ajar, but we couldn't see or hear a thing.

"I'm not going in. We'll get in trouble."

"No we won't. Nobody'll see us."

> (The worms crawl in
> The worms crawl out
> The worms play pinochle on your snout...)

Jane gave the door a little push. It swung open and she went inside, then stuck her head out and whispered, "It's all right. There's nobody in here."

I wanted to run away — quickly — but Jane would call me a baby if I didn't go in. It was very dark inside and smelled funny, like our house when we came back at the end of summer. Only damp, too, and evil.

What if the caretaker saw the door open and didn't bother to look inside, just shut it up and walked away? The walls were very thick and nobody would hear us pounding. We'd die there in the darkness when the air was all used up. Who'd bother to search for us in a mausoleum? Mother would think the perverts had gotten us.

Some stranger passing through town would be accused,

arrested, electrocuted at Sing Sing because of us. Some wandering Jew, some moon-faced boy with newspapers stuffed in his shoes, sitting in the shadows under the railway bridge, waiting to hop a train.

"That's him. I know it. You can see it in his eyes."

Maybe Jane really wanted to die, the way I did sometimes, and was going to shut us both in here because she was fed up with being alive. I began to cry and found it difficult to catch my breath.

"Let's go back."

"Don't be a baby."

"Please, come out of here. I want to go back!" It might be some kind of a sin and God would strike us dead. Or against the law.

TRESPASSERS WILL BE PROSECUTED.

"Please." I hung on tight to the door.

"Shut up." (And Jane's whisper came back from the walls as though all those dead people were whispering shut up shut up shut up which is what they were and what we would be too.)

"I want to go home!"

But how could I leave without Jane, who was moving along the aisle looking at all the metal plaques fixed on to the walls. Some light came in from a high grilled window, and now that we were used to the darkness it was possible to make out the writing on the plaques. It was like a huge filing cabinet in there, and the dead people were all in drawers, one on top of the other. There were names on all but two.

"Look," whispered Jane. "Melissa, '1902-1920!' she was only eighteen! I wonder what happened to her?"

It was awful to think of Melissa in there with her long hair and long pointy fingernails. Shut up Shut up Shut up.

"Let's go."

"All right."

The door swung quietly back in place and I thought the world had never looked so beautiful. I wanted to lie down and roll over and over in the good green grass, to take great swallows of fresh air and lie face upward in the sun. Thank you god thank you o thank you. I'll never be naughty again.

We walked casually down the path, willing ourselves not to hurry. But there was a woman a few graves down who gave us a funny look and seemed about to call out, so Jane said loudly, "Poor dear Aunt Harriet. I'm so glad we came to pay our last respects." And as soon as we got beyond the trees we ran like crazy back to Daddy and Mother, who had been looking all over for us. We'd have to hurry and have lunch or we wouldn't be ready when Harry came to pick us up and take us out to put flowers on Ga-Ga's grave that afternoon.

I knelt on the back seat and watched the cemetery growing smaller and smaller in the rear-view mirror. My mother's mirror-eye caught mine.

"Sit properly!"

Then Jane said, "Poor dear Aunt Harriet" very low and we both got the giggles all the way home.

But the other cemetery was really my favourite. Out through the town on Highway 7, past Conklin and under the railway culvert where my father, if he were driving, leaned hard on his horn and the sound echoed all around us, booming, honk-honk-honk, like geese, warning any cars coming from the other direction that here we were and they'd just better wait until we were through (there was room for only a single car at a time). To Goodenough, nothing now but a few houses, the cemetery, a rundown general store, a church, but once a small thriving village when my great-grandfather and his son ran the now abandoned acid factory. Everything was dust-coloured and decaying, and although Harry paid a local man to scythe the grass, it was usually long and fragrant, full of Jack-in-the-pulpits and lady slippers and columbines; buttercups and a curious plant with rubbery leaves that Harry taught us to blow up, like green balloons. Many of the gravestones here were tiny sheep, marking the place where a child lay, often stillborn or only a few weeks old. Considering my fear of death, this should have frightened me; but the weather-beaten lambs, almost hidden in the tall grass, seemed at home there in that rundown place, more field than cemetery, and I had a great affection for them. Three of the lambs belonged to Harry and my grandmother: Frances and Benjamin (twins) and Eleanor. That was why Ga-Ga had been so delicate. Your grandfather never... My sister and I dumped out the wilted flowers and rust-coloured water from our last visit and refilled jam jars with fresh water from the creek below the cemetery. "Be careful! Don't fall in." Then we made up new bouquets for the dead babies or sat in the grass and wove daisy chains. Harry and Ga-Ga had a single tombstone, like Grandpa and Grandma Cleary, but Harry's inscription was incomplete, 1868—. My mother usually brought cut flowers from a florist. They came in a special plaster-board container with a long stake on the end of it. You shoved the stake into the ground and that made me uneasy, too, like my father digging holes for his geraniums. Afterward we would drive to the end of the road and visit Harry's cousin, a very old lady named Aunt Deveena who lived with Cousin Alfred and Muriel Clapp. We sat on the porch in the sun and drank raspberry vinegar and shouted at the old lady through her ornate ear trumpet, black with silver chasing, which seemed so out of place with her feed-sack print dresses and her nephew's overalls. She was nearly a hundred years old and I don't think she understood a word we said. But smiled and twinkled and commanded Cousin Muriel to "bring out some more of them sugar biscuits for the young'uns." As we ate and drank, gigantic sunflowers lolled their idiot heads beside the house. I wanted to ask her what it felt like to be so close to death; but her merry eyes dared me to ask such a damn-fool question, and we went away with only the usual remarks having passed. My mother always said "Isn't she wonderful!" to Cousin Muriel, a dour, heavyset woman in her sixties, and my father always said "You can't beat home-made country cookin'" or something equally bland. Aunt Deveena lived to be a hundred and got her picture on the front section of the *Press*.

"That side of the family always was long-lived," said my mother absently, and I, who at that time had reached a new low in despair and depression, wondered if my particular curse would turn out to be, after all, not a sudden death but a long, long life. I stared at Aunt Deveena and her birthday cake, Alfred on one side of her chair, Muriel on the other, and wondered how one kept on, day after day, for a century.

But still I said rabbit, rabbit, rabbit if I passed a cemetery on the first day of the month.

My other grandmother, Ga-Ga, Harry's wife, I remembered hardly at all. I thought of her later more in terms of touch and smell than as a person with a face and body. She had been ailing for some time when Harry planned and built the cottage, and whether Journey's End was a particularly brutal joke or whether he did not realize how very ill she was was never settled. She went to the cottage in our very early years, and there are photographs of her and Harry in sailor hats, holding large, stupid-eyed fish heads downward, or with oars held up like spears ready to set off on some expedition or other. But I, Isobel, remembered my grandmother in the mountains only in terms of the large leather-covered horsehair sofa in the great central room and the gay orange crocheted afghan under which she lay. Ga-Ga smelled of lavender water, and her hair was soft and fine like the angel hair on the Christmas tree. She wore a beautiful little enamel brooch with harebells painted on it. But her voice was querulous with fatigue and pain, and the one sentence I remember clearly is "For heaven's sake take that child down to the lake, I *can not rest*." Jane, who was older and quieter, would be allowed to stay by her grandmother and look through the wonderful old stereopticon at coloured scenes of Venice or London which, with careful adjustment of the crosspiece, would leap out suddenly in thrilling three-dimensionality. I resented this favouritism tremendously and would run out and cling possessively to one of Harry's massive legs until, if he were busy (and he usually was), he would be forced to pull me off like a tick. Once, when I could have been no older than four, I ran off by myself, in a temper, and flung myself across the hot sand, shouting, "You wait. You just wait. Someday I'll go to all those places and leave you all behind." When I was about to set off for Europe the first time, Harry told me this story and told me how they had all laughed at the little wild thing on the beach with its grandiose ideas. Told me and slipped me twenty dollars.

"You laughed too?"

"Why, sure." (He was over eighty then.) "Even Mother. We all did." I thanked him for the money, but I never spent it and Isobel has it still.

It was probably the following winter that my grandmother died. I was in "kindergarten A" (afternoons) and we had planned a concert and party to which all the parents (this meant mothers) and relatives (this meant aunts or grand-mothers) were invited. Kindergarten had been the first great change in my life and I reacted to it with a mixture of hate and love. I loved the drums and triangles and tambourines, the big boxes of crayons and the endless supply of paper. I loved the bright clean room with its large windows and pictures every-where. I even, at first, loved Mrs. Behan, the kindergarten teacher. But I hated the other children, who seemed so much larger (my mother had fought with the school superintendent to let me start school although I was only four) and more knowl-edgeable of the customs of kindergartens and playgrounds. I struggled to learn to tie my laces — and failed. I struggled to make friends with the other little girls — and failed again. The boys I simply could not cope with. They undid the bows on my dresses, pulled my pigtails, hid behind trees with angleworms or icy snowballs in their strong, masculine paws. And once, when I had to go to the bathroom suddenly, I ran out of the room with-out holding up my finger and waiting for permission — a public gesture that I found shameful and disgusting anyway. The teacher was very cross with me and made me sit by myself when it was time for rhythm band. So that the next time I neither left the room nor held up my hand and had to be taken home, wet through and crying horribly, by my disgusted (grade two) sister. After that, through a perverse logic of my own, I hated Mrs. Behan and never volunteered to help clean up the room although my heart yearned toward the hoary erasers which could be taken outside and banged together until a great cloud of dust, like silent, aerated music, rose above my head; toward the shiny blunt-beaked scissors, the twenty-five varicoloured pencils to be sharpened and made ready for the following afternoon. And after that I exerted my will to such an extent that it was a matter of dark pride with me that I never had to hold my fingers up again, although my mother, seeing my customary dash upstairs for the bathroom when I came home, warned me repeatedly of the dire consequences of a "burst bladder," a thing I imagined in such graphic and disgusting terms I knew it would never happen to me. I'd slit my throat instead.

But that afternoon — the afternoon of the concert — Mrs. Behan made us all line up in twos and marched us to the lavatories twenty minutes before the concert was to begin. Boys on the left side of the hall, to the boys' toilets, girls on the right. Our teacher stood in the middle, androgynous, tapping her foot impatiently and darting into one toilet or the other (usually the boys') if the allotted group did not come out in what she considered sufficient time. I had a new dress to wear, teal green velveteen, with an enormous and rather scratchy white collar. It was a gift from one of the downstate aunts, and I was especially privileged to be allowed to wear it before Christmas. I also had a new pair of patent-leather Mary Janes and was constantly licking my hanky and polishing them. Each child had made gifts, all more or less identical: half a paper plate stitched in red or green wool to a whole paper plate, then the rather grubby artifact lavishly decorated with Christmas stickers or pictures cut from ladies' magazines. These presents were to be used for bills or recipes and were to be presented after the singing and refreshments. Both my mother and Ga-Ga had promised to come, and I was in agony of suspense — we all were — during the first hour when school — ridiculous thought — was to "go on as usual." How could it *possibly*, with mounds of Christmas cookies and little sandwiches over there on the table, never mind that they were covered up with tea towels? When there was a special crate of chocolate milk just outside the door? When the classroom smelled of pine from the handsome tree, overdecorated by all of us, by the piano? The back of my head felt curiously heavy because my hair, for once, had been left unbraided. I dreamed my way through the adventures of Big C and little c, through counting and word identification. "Tree." "Lights." "Present." It was all very easy anyway. I kept glancing at my painting of a great, glittering Christmas tree, secretly pleased that the teacher had liked it well enough to hang it above the blackboard.

At two o'clock we could hear doors opening and shutting, a shuffling outside in the corridor. Discreet coughs and the murmur of voices. We fidgeted, knowing it was nearly time. When *at last* Mrs. Behan opened the classroom doors and ushered the grownups to the rows of chairs which had been borrowed from the auditorium, I think we were all in a terrible state of pleasure and embarrassment. Red-faced and solemn, we sat in a semicircle around the piano and eyed our relatives, acknowledging smiles and waves with stiff, embarrassed grimaces. I saw my mother, eyes blinking from the cold, come in with my grandmother and sit down near the windows. I gazed at the other children's mothers, aunts, grandmothers — a very few uncomfortable fathers — and tried to assimilate the fact that all these large, alien, noisy beings were related by blood to my classmates. It was too much, and I turned away to contemplate our teacher, pink-cheeked and almost pretty with self-importance. She slowly glanced around the room, seemed satisfied, and sat down at the piano. She played a loud chord. Some of the grownups kept on talking and we giggled nervously to think our elders did not know, or did not REMEMBER, what a loud chord meant.

"Shh," said Mary Lou Whelan, who had naturally curly hair and had been told she looked like Shirley Temple. "Mith Behan ith gonna begin."

"Oh, isn't she *sweet*" chirped the mothers. And then, laughing self-consciously, settled down.

We sang all the old favourites, "sweetly" for "Silent Night," "with gusto" for "Jingle Bells." We forgot our parents and moved and breathed as one organism, hypnotized by our teacher's hands at the piano, by the old myth in which we still so fervently believed. I loved singing, and for the first time since I had entered school I felt at peace — one with the other starched and slicked-up creatures with whom I now shared my days. One, even, with my avowed enemy, the teacher, whose hands could make such magic fill the room. I was nearly unconscious with joy and well-being. The great tree by the piano seemed to reach out its spicy fingers and enter into some very secret part of me of which, until now, I had been totally unaware. It was with surprise and almost physical shock that I realized the teacher had stopped playing, that we had all stopped singing, that sandwiches and cookies and bottles of milk had appeared miraculously and were being passed around. I wanted to remain with the music, within that strange enchanted semicircle, forever. But I felt more at ease now and waved to my mother and grandmother, who were leaning over and talking to Mrs. Drainie, mother of the nastiest boy in the class. In my newfound happiness I could even wave at Mrs. Drainie and forgive her for ever having borne such a fat and sadistic child. I ate my cookie, a large bell with impossibly pink icing, and sucked noisily at the bottom of my milk bottle like all the others.

Now the children chosen to be helpers packed the bottles neatly away in their crate, collected tea cups and saucers, offered the few remaining sandwiches and cookies for the third and final time (Ronald Drainie had the audacity to grab two and was given a playful tap by the teacher) and then sat down with the others for the presents. For practical reasons the children would receive theirs (piled under the Christmas tree) at the end of the afternoon. The teacher began by moving forward a card table on which were stacked about twenty-five identical objects done up in red or green tissue paper. She looked coyly at the tag on the first parcel.

"Now let me see. 'Merry Christmas to Mommy from Helen.' Well! Will Helen's mommy come forward, please?" We giggled with excitement as Helen's mommy detached herself from the other adults and came forward, rather awkwardly (as though she, too, were under the influence of the teacher), and accepted her gift. There were many "oh"s and "ah"s and "how clever"s as Helen's mommy undid the package with great ceremony and held up the bill collector/recipe holder for all to see. "Thank you very much, dear," she said, and everyone dutifully clapped.

Naturally the novelty of this wore off. Peter's mommy, Mary Lou's mommy, Ronald's mommy — each went forward and received her gift with varying degrees of pride, embarrassment and awkwardness; each gathered "oh"s and "ah"s, said "thank you, dear" and garnered polite applause. But we were growing restless. Those whose gifts had already been received were especially noisy and several more playful taps had to be given out by a somewhat harassed Mrs. Behan. The teacher began to speed up. "Let's have two this time. Anne's mommy and Joseph's mommy." I wondered if my turn would ever come. I had worked hard and made two — one for Ga-Ga as well since she was taking the trouble to come. Yet I was worried because I had done this and wondered if the other kids or their parents would laugh and if maybe I should have left well enough alone. The teacher was near the end now and the room was very noisy. I needed to go to the bathroom. Suddenly there was a strange "thump" — the sound of a chair tipping over — and a single cry, "Mother!"

At first I didn't recognize the voice. I was too much involved in my own fears and anticipations. Mrs. Behan had stopped reading and was hurrying to the back of the room. Someone said, "Stand back, give her room." Someone else said, "Oh. How terrible." A man's voice said, "I'll phone for the ambulance." The children, alarmed, deserted by their teacher, started milling about. threatened to stampede. One boy broke through the wall of adult backs and came back frightened and excited. "Somebody's granny is lyin' on the floor." Several of the little girls began to whimper.

I sat as cold and motionless as stone. Knew without being told whose granny it was, whose granny it had to be. The festive atmosphere had dissolved in a flash, and I was all alone and alien once more. I could hear, through the noise, the dreadful sound of my mother, crying, "Mother oh Mother Mother oh my Mother."

Mrs. Behan hurried back to the piano. "Now, children, there's been a little accident but everything's going to be fine. We'll have a little singsong while we're waiting for things to settle down." She struck a *very* loud chord. I could tell that she was furious that such a thing should have happened in *her* class and at *her* concert.

"Jingle bells, jingle bells, jingle all the way." She sang loudly and compellingly but the children remained silent. She whirled around on her stool.

"Now. Now. Where have all my good children gone? Out the window? We'll begin again." Then she hissed, "Sing." They, true at last to their general, sang. The parents still presented a solid barrier behind us, but we were all aware of the sound of a siren, of the fact that something had come in and something heavy and unconscious had been taken out. I heard the long ribbon of my mother's sobbing unwind down the corridor. Mrs. Behan kept on, "I saw three ships come sailing in, sailing in, sailing in." Hypnotized, we sang. There was a nervous giggle. Mary Lou.

"Pleath, Mith Behan."

"What is it *now*," hissed the teacher, still playing and not turning around.

"Pleath. Ithobel hath wet all over the floor."

My grandmother did not actually die until the next morning. Jane and I were taken home by Mrs. Drainie, where we had to endure the manifold tortures of Ronald, who was looking particularly grotesque due to surgical clips in his forehead, and eat strange exotic food for supper. And I, ultimate indignity, had to wear a pair of Ronald's underpants. Our father came for us late at night and we went to bed without brushing our teeth or saying our prayers. We cuddled up to each other in the same bed and decided to pray for Ga-Ga ourselves. I prayed long and earnestly — and meant it. But one part of me knew I would never forgive my grandmother, who was supposed to have been a lady, for having had the bad taste to have a heart attack at my kindergarten Christmas party. To fall backward out of her chair like some circus acrobat. It was too much. I felt as though my life at school was over.

We didn't go to the funeral. Mother decided we were too young and easily upset. I heard her say to Aunt Olive, who had called to say she was sorry, "If only I hadn't persuaded her to go out that day — it seemed to mean so much to Isobel."

Which was worse, Isobel? The sound of the key from the inside, locking her in, or sitting downstairs or waiting in your bedroom for the key to turn again? When she might burst out like a circus animal, like the real Grace Poole, roaring, biting, eager to attack.

Or when she called us all together and laughed her little laugh and asked us to forget?

three

We moved into my grandmother's house when Uncle Pudge's family was transferred to Oneonta. Grandma Cleary had gone by ambulance and Jane and I watched through the front room curtains as the ambulance attendants slid the stretcher in the back, fitting it in neatly, like a bread pan on an oven rack, and closing the double doors. Aunt Catherine got up front with the driver. Uncle Pudge would follow in the De Soto with the two girls. The Mayflower Moving Van had come the day before, piling in the old, dark furniture, Grandma's wheelchair, the twin beds and vanity table that belonged to our two cousins, steamer trunks, chairs and the dining room table.

We would not have a van — it was only next door, after all; some movers would come in the afternoon to help shift the heavier pieces. I knew the neighbours would see our shabbiness and was embarrassed by the whole ridiculous performance. The move itself simply confirmed my already mature suspicions that we would never do anything in the ordinary way, would always be set off from other people and behave in a manner that appeared bizarre in the world's eyes as well as my own. Whoever heard of moving next door to yourself? It was no move at all. And to such a house! It was because Auntie O. would let us have it dirt cheap and we were up to our ears, as usual. I understood but I did not accept. Just as I understood but did not accept why my sister and I were taken down to the First City National to negotiate or renegotiate a loan. Our parents in their shabby clothes (Mother's hair already escaping from its pins, the heels of her good pumps worn down to the wood; our father's collar frayed and his hat band stained inside with Vaseline) might confirm the impression given by their bank account, but the children...! There were the bright, shining children to think of. No sacrifice was too great. Sometimes our report cards were brought along or the Bible I had won at Religious Instruction. We were used to the cool eyes of assistant managers and knew how to look both determined and grateful. Except for the bank manager himself, all the personnel worked in open, carpeted areas in full view of the public. Their neat suits and oak desks were impressive. So were my mother's tears, if she chose to use them. Upstairs on the mezzanine, Mr. Gilmore, the father of one of my classmates, could look down on the whole charade. What hanky-panky could possibly go on?

The move to our grandmother's house was just one more humiliation. We knew the house already, hated and feared it; for our families, although separated only by two pear trees, a quince apple bush and the old garage, never spoke if we could avoid it. Yet every Sunday for as along as we could remember we had been taken to visit the old lady in the upstairs back bedroom which she never left and which smelled of something like cat but not quite cat (I did not, then, recognize the smell of sickness and old age). She was terribly crippled with arthritis, had claws for hands and her head set at an impossible angle, as though she were listening to secret messages from her shoulder. When she spoke it was in a high, faraway voice from the back of her throat, a thin vibrato which reminded me of the voices on the cylindrical wax records we played on an old wind-up Victrola, the only possession of my father's in which I took any real interest. Like those voices, my grandmother's voice seemed to come from beyond the grave.

Uncle Pudge would open the door and say a few words to his brother. They looked alike. Both had round bellies and weak, friendly, boyish faces. Then he would disappear, leaving us to find our own way up the dingy stairs and down the dingy corridor to their mother's room. We were aware of our aunt and cousins only as breathings behind closed doors. The feud had gone on a long time and had something to do with Aunt Caroline, who was an RC, and something to do (of course) with money. We were not allowed to kiss our grandmother either. But not because of the feud. You never knew what you might catch. Not that we wanted to — it was enough to have to touch those frozen hands.

When I was old enough to read Dickens I could understand Pip's horror at the sight of Miss Havisham and his disgust at the decay of her old mansion. But what really sent a dark thrill down my back was the scene in which Pip finally kisses the dying old woman on the lips. I knew that if Jane or I kissed our grandmother on the lips *we* would surely die.

And now we were living in our grandmother's house, and somebody else, a new family named Leuss ("What kind of a name is that?" said our mother angrily) had replaced us in the other house. Daddy was obviously happy to be back in the house where he was born. ("See those floors? Solid oak they are. You don't get hardwood floors like that in your houses any more.") Even took over the upstairs back bedroom and replaced his mother's smell with his: cigarette tobacco and stale sheets. The dresser was covered with little bits of tobacco and the matchbooks which he had been collecting for years and always meant to cut up and put away in albums. Dust and that year's red diary in which he wrote faithfully every day.

> "Sunday: March 6. Cold and sunny.
> A few daffs coming up. Drove out to
> the David Harum for Chicken Fricassee."

46

By the time of his death there was a small pile of these diaries in one corner of the room, covered in dust like everything else, and I went through them earnestly, looking for some statement of joy or pain, some peg on which I could finally hang the terrible weight of my indifference and contempt. I found nothing. Just temperatures, dates, notes about his flowers or fishing trips. Endless columns of figures. I could see the two blue spruce he had planted, as a child, out the back room window. But if the diaries were a code it was one I did not know how to break, and in the end I left the books there in the corner, along with his Knights Templar uniform and his fishing reel, for my mother to dispose of. My childhood memories of him and his untidy, smelly room could still arouse distaste fifteen years later. He rarely bathed, maintaining it "sapped your strength." Rarely cut his toenails. Hated and feared the dentist. "Look here," he would say when I was ten or eleven or so, "ee air is ooth ish goan," his pudgy finger forcing his lower lip down and back to reveal a decayed and broken molar. He had one dentist he trusted, out in Port Dickenson, and when things really got too bad he would take himself off there and "get fixed up." Mother would snort contemptuously and refer to Dr. Slocan as "that old fool!" and "a waste of good money," although probably no money had ever changed hands.

So our father came back to his mother's room where he was born. It led down a corridor and through to the upstairs hall, so that if he closed his door and the hall door he was pretty well cut off from the rest of the house. We could hear him in there at night, pacing up and down while he practised out loud for a new Masonic degree, or often, in the middle of the night, wheezing and gasping with another attack of asthma. He had trouble with his digestion as well, would take Sal Hepatica and lock himself in the bathroom. Afterward I couldn't bear it if I had to go in. The place stank and the window had been, years ago, painted shut.

I felt very little but contempt and disgust. He was weak both physically and morally; he could not provide. When he occasionally tried to assert himself by saying we'd all end up on the

State Farm, Mother would quickly chop him down. What about his fancy duds for the Masons, his new fishing reel, last night's porterhouse steaks? They argued in the dining room or kitchen with the door shut "because of the children." Their anger rose like vapour through the hot-air registers.

Our mother slept separately, in one of the two front bedrooms overlooking the street. She was just as untidy as our father. Her chest of drawers was filled with boxes of unfinished sewing and candy boxes full of old photographs and greeting cards. Spilled face powder. Stockings that needed mending. Indeed, the whole house was soon like this, our layers just added to the junk that was left behind.

The chaos began in the basement, down steep, ill-lighted stairs which led down from the kitchen. There was also a short flight of steps leading directly in from the backyard and a coal window facing the driveway where the Blue Coal man used to dump the winter coal into a little coal cellar before we converted to gas. In an old pantry off the main room two rows of jars filled with poisonous-looking shapes in a dull red liquid (beets? pickled human hearts?) stood where they most probably had been put at least a quarter century before. I tried to imagine my Grandma Cleary's hands managing anything as complicated as the awkward spring contraptions which kept the glass lids on.

Also in the cellar two old wicker baby carriages, heavy ancient bread pans with ridged, hinged lids for making cylindrical loaves on some far-off forgotten wood stove. A pair of skis (one broken), cans of paint with their lids gummed up, most likely forever, and yellow newspapers, mouse-eaten, advertising Grandpa Cleary's dry goods and hardware store and steak at fifteen cents a pound. The garden hose. The lawnmower. Broken terra-cotta flower pots. Always, in the winter, on some dusty box or other, a flat blue bowl filled with hyacinths or paper narcissus which my father was "forcing" for Easter. Enormous archetypal spider webs with dead flies in them but no spiders. Storm windows. Mice pellets on the floor. The gas furnace went on with a terrible thump and the hot air rushed up the metal arms like frantic ghosts. It was a pretty scary place to be.

Upstairs, recipes that would never be used were cut out and shoved into drawers. Bills, bills, bills, some of them underlined in red. Old Christmas cards. Stacks of jar lids. A beautiful broken fan with ivory ribs. Razor blades and candle ends. A single artificial fingernail.

(Under our beds upstairs, nestled among the dust kitties, dress boxes full of party dresses: taffeta, Thai silk, velveteen, belonging to Jane or myself. Hat boxes containing Easter hats.)

Drawers would not shut or would not open. Ceilings fell down on our heads. Open windows suddenly slammed shut. Fuses blew (it seemed) of their own accord. Our grandmother's house had a Dickensian vitality of its own. When we were teenagers and the Collier mansion with its two dead old men and mountains of newspaper was discovered, we all had a good laugh and nicknamed our house "The Collier Mansion." (In the attic, *Life* magazines and *National Geographics*, locked cabin trunks with no keys, an unfinished sampler:

"GOD BLESS OUR HO—"

At the same time a sliver of fear caught at my heart. To end like that, suffocated by the past! Meanwhile Daddy smoked his Lucky Strikes and coughed and practised his speeches and maybe did unmentionable things into his pocket handkerchiefs. Mother sat on our beds for a little talk or locked us out of the house until we had said, enough times, we're sorry sorry sorry.

That night would appear the twenty-page letter on the yellow stenographer's paper she used to keep her "hand in." Reiterating the family history since the time of our great-great-grandfather's departure from England with his wife and seven children, in a small packet boat, right up to the present day and beyond, into the dark satanic future unless we changed our ways. In these letters would also be explained the reasons why she was striving to keep the family together, "in spite of everything," and how we must never sell ourselves short in life. After the days on which there was a letter (sometimes one to each of us, sometimes one for us to share), there would be something special for supper and maybe Floating Island for dessert or pie from the German bakery.

I was ten years old and in the fifth grade before I discovered the uncomfortable fact that husbands and wives often slept together in the same bed and in the same bedroom.

So it seemed only fitting, however much we hated it, that we should live in the spiritual squalor of our grandmother's house. All the wallpaper had faded to a uniform yellow-brown, whatever the original design. There was sheet linoleum in the kitchen and upstairs hall, worn through to the gummy black backing in places, even through to the layers of old yellowed newspaper which had been put underneath for padding. Our world was brown and stained with damp, like the wallpaper or the nasty crack in the bathroom basin, or our hair, which refused to curl the way our mother hoped it would. Brown with slashes of red (anger) — our own or that of our parents. I wrote secret letters to movie stars:

Dear Robert Walker,
I am eleven years old and very unhappy.
Dear Judy Garland,
I read poetry and stay after school.

My sister had a girlfriend down the street. I played with them sometimes but longed for a friend of my own. Occasionally I tried, at school, but I had no real idea how to go about it, and the world of my classmates seemed so removed, however desirable, that I found the burden of my family too heavy to try and share. My mother darned socks so that they came up in hateful little lumps which showed and rubbed against my heels. My Brownie uniform was secondhand, of a different style and lighter colour, and yet I had more party dresses than I had parties to go to. Our mother didn't belong to the Monday Afternoon Club nor our father to the Chamber of Commerce or Country Club. But it was more than just this. There was something as foul as the stopped drains, the long brown crack in the bathroom basin, that went on at our house. Mother equated her misery with lack of "station" and "nice things." And, being my mother's daughter, I did this too. Some days I felt that if I could *only* have a wristwatch with a leather strap, or a pair of shorts from Best & Co., the world would come out right again. But my older, wiser self suspected that this was not so. We had not learned, in the Presbyterian Sunday school, the real meaning behind the story of Cain and Abel; but I sensed, nevertheless, that my sister and I carried a certain mark upon our foreheads, clearly visible to all the other children, which set us irrevocably apart. We would never be killed, but neither would we be befriended.

If we were invited to another child's house — to work on a project about the winter sky, perhaps, yoked together with a reluctant Cathy or Heather or Jeanette, because of a lack of resource books — it was an awkward time for everyone concerned. My mother was sure I was about to be "taken up" by Cathy (after all, hadn't she and Grace been members of ΦΚ together, years ago?) and I was lectured on how to behave, dressed in my best pleated skirt and twin set, my newest pair of glen-plaid slacks. Cathy would open the door in blue jeans and her brother's sweatshirt. Cathy's mother would say a vague "hello dear how are you Cathy dear show Isobel where to hang her jacket" and retreat to the kitchen, where she was making cookies or deveining shrimp for a Saturday evening dinner party. Cathy and I would go up to her bedroom (matching chintz bedspread, drapes, vanity table, a reproduction of Van Gogh's "Sunflowers," perhaps, above the bed) and get to work with our blue construction paper and white ink, copying out parts of the winter constellation. Cathy had wall-to-wall carpeting on her bedroom floor and a collection of bronze-metal figurines of horses. She did not need to open her cupboards or drawers to demonstrate the neatness and order I yearned for. At five o'clock her mother would remind her that she had to have a bath before the company came, and I, the intruder, would wait downstairs in the hall for my father goddamn him who had promised to be there on time.

On Monday, when the Social Studies project was handed in, my paper would seem terribly smudged and blurred, as though it had smudged and blurred itself, on purpose, while Cathy's would be held up by the teacher as "the sort of thing I was looking for."

Once, at one of these houses, the girl I was working with took me down to the kitchen for a Coke and a look at the Christmas spritz cookies her mother had been baking. She told me to take a chew of a shiny white thing that lay on the kitchen counter. It was a clove of garlic. My friend laughed and laughed while I ran coatless and hatless from the house, even knowing as I ran and wept that I would have to return on my own or my mother, always looking for opportunity, would cause a fearful row. My mouth tasted foul for days. By the time I graduated from elementary school I felt I knew all there was to know about the cruelty of adults and of children. It did not surprise me that there was a war on and that men would want to kill with guns as well as words.

Then, when I was in seventh grade, I came home one day to discover the hall and sitting room full of huge cardboard boxes. Mother — flushed and girlish; even her voice seemed to have taken on a girlish lilt — appeared from the kitchen, wiping her hands. There was a smell of celebration and roast beef in the air.

"We're going to change a few things, honey," she said. "Your grandma's estate's been settled."

Together with Jane, we ripped open the cartons with kitchen knives, spilling out sheets and pillowcases and candlewick bedspreads in green and cream and rose. Gold and rose brocaded sateen for downstairs drapes and some carpet was coming tomorrow. We were allowed to choose new wallpaper for our rooms.

(Downstairs a cherrywood chair, Provincial style, a sofa in Regency stripe, two end tables in cherrywood and two rather exotic lamps, bisque chinamen with rose organza lampshades growing out of their hats. A vacuum cleaner in an imitation-leather hassock. Two men from the Sally Ann came around for the old stuff but said they weren't sure it could be fixed up.

"I don't know, lady. If it don't have any resale value we ain't supposed to take it.")

I was skeptical at first. Any past attempt to "fix things up" always seemed to misfire. But lulled by the sudden lack of arguments and the ocular proof of the "things" that kept appearing at the door (such a wealth of delivery trucks — it was unbelievable!), I began to plan the renovation of my room. Not wall-to-wall carpet, of course, but it could look nice. I lay on my bed and thought very seriously about it. About primary colours — an army of reds and yellows and blues to push back the browns of the past. Colours like band music; colours like summer sunshine and impossible blue skies and a hundred red convertibles.

Yet in the end I decided on pastels as more appropriate to myself. Old Rose and French Grey. It was the names in the wallpaper book that decided me. I would have the rose bedspread mother had bought "on approval" and a rose scatter rug. My sister chose flowered chintz in green and white. And in due time an old man came, Mr. Stofer, whose wife was dead and who brought a quart of milk with him each day, which he drank at one go halfway through the morning. He wore a white painter's cap with a green visor and old white overalls which had a brownish, discoloured seat as though he had messed himself and the stain had never come out. I was a little afraid of him — he smelled of damp and sweat and plaster — but was enthralled at the way he changed the tiny box room at the head of the stairs, a room I had hated both for its position (the murderers, ghosts and rapists would get me first) and pokiness, into my room, three walls grey and one wall rose.

After he had moved on to do the hall I painted the old chest and a bookcase and the night table grey and splatter-painted them with rose enamel, carefully putting down newspapers right to the edge of the floor. I had seen some splatter-painted tables in the Hotel Ten Eyck Coffee Shoppe, on our one trip to the state capital, and had vowed that someday I would to do that to my furniture. It was so strange at last to be able to take these three desperate pieces of cast-off furniture, the dull green bookcase, the old maple night table, the white chest of drawers with some of the drawer pulls missing, and turn them into a composite whole. The grey came out a little darker than I had hoped, but it didn't really matter. A box-spring mattress and Hollywood headboard appeared; percale sheets so white and perfect in their newness I was afraid to use them and then contaminate them in the family washing machine. I knew, as did Jane, that the milk bill hadn't been paid, the Blue Cross was overdue, the telephone might be cut off at any minute (the voices were coming up the registers again; Daddy had asthma nearly every night); but by now we were so carried away with our own particular visions of our new rooms that it didn't matter any more. (French grey, old rose: colours beyond primary, the more suitable colours of June roses and April skies. Soft. Rain-washed. Safe.)

When it was all finished, when my throw rug had been tried first beside the bed, then at the foot of it; when the framed copy of Kipling's "If" (a long-ago present from Aunt Hettie) had been hung on a nail over my bed and my few books had been put in the bookcase, there was still the matter of the naked bulb which hung like a memory or an accusation from the bedroom wall. I got a lampshade but then it seemed too dark. What I really needed, I decided, was a pair of lamps for the chest of drawers cum dressing table. I asked my mother (a new suite of cherrywood furniture had appeared in the near front bedroom; drapes were being made on the new sewing machine; there was a dining table covered in glass, of all things, a set of silverplate, a set of Syracuse china) and my mother said "of course." This time I asked to go downtown by myself. (Mr. Stofer had done the hall in lords and ladies, the kitchen in washable Dutch blue and white. Only our father's room remained the same.)

It took my entire Saturday morning and ten dollars to find what wanted. All the way home on the bus I cradled the box in my lap; inside were the lamps, which would be the final touch. I nearly stumbled getting off, and my chest hurt with the knowledge of what might have happened.

Up the street to our house and then back to the hardware store for an extension cord ("white, please"). The lamps were cream-coloured (Jane said "why yellow?" but she was wrong) and had pale cream lampshades. That night I lay in the golden light and felt, for the first time in that terrible house, a kind of sensuous peace. There were venetian blinds and white organdy curtains. I no longer had to look over into the Leuss' bedroom unless I chose. The old cracked green window shade had been set out for the garbage man in the morning. I took a bath and washed my hair and slipped naked between the sheets, saying a small prayer for my grandmother because I felt rather guilty about enjoying the benefits of her money and yet refusing to attend (last year) her funeral. There had not been enough paper for the inside of the cupboard, but I had straightened my clothes, arranging them in order on the bamboo pole that served as closet rod. Dusted the boxes piled above and vowed to keep the door shut whenever possible.

The following week I invited Cathy and Heather and Jeanette to come over and see my room on a Saturday afternoon. I made Toll House cookies in the morning and made sure there was enough milk. I even cleaned the toilet. At three o'clock they still hadn't come. At four my mother called up, "Well, are your fancy friends coming to see you or not?" At five I shut my door and wished I had a key, like Mother's, to lock it once for all.

Monday morning, in the cloakroom, Heather said, "Oh, hi. Sorry about Saturday. We played tennis instead. I tried to call you but the operator said your line was 'temporarily disconnected'." Cathy giggled into her hand. ("We never noticed," I thought. "We never picked up the phone.")

Jeanette said, adjusting her Alice band, "Maybe we'll get around to it this weekend."

"Yeah," said Cathy and Heather together, anxious to get out of the way.

"Don't bother," I said. "Just damn well don't bother."

The curtains my mother made were measured wrong and one drape was far too short. It was hung behind the edge of the piano, our grandmother's piano, which nobody ever played. The money was all gone very soon, and Daddy spilled a cup of coffee on the Regency striped sofa. The phone was connected again, eventually, but it didn't seem to matter. Nobody called but the bill collectors or my sister's boyfriends.

"God," I whispered from inside my perfect bedroom, "please let me die."

four

"Isobel," she said, "you're cold, your heart's a stone." She stood behind me, holding my head and forcing me to look in the mirror.

"Look at you. Look at your face. Look at it!"

I learned to disconnect myself early, to leave my body and stand outside, above really, looking downward at Clara holding Isobel. Why did she hate us so? Perhaps we were a constant affront to her, the awkward and visible proof to herself, as well as to Harry, the neighbours, society at large, that she had been intimate with this FAILURE, this lame excuse for a man. This may also have led her to a total denial of his masculinity through her many hints to us that he was "perverted," a homosexual or homosexually inclined. I once found a box of Norforms in his dresser drawer and had the idea he stuck them up himself for pleasure. The sexual act itself, in spite of my mother's hints, in spite of the neighbourhood dogs, remained incomprehensible to me. We lived, the four of us, in a house where the body was virtually denied any existence — certainly any pleasant one. I never consciously masturbated. It was beyond my powers of imagination. Bodies were ugly, shameful things — "Isobel, pull your skirt down," "Jane, sit up properly." She had a curious phrase for any glimpse of our private parts, covered or uncovered. "Put your legs together, Isobel, I don't want to have my picture taken." She talked of so and so being "over-sexed" or "too sexy" and once told us, in one of her many unsolicited, unwanted confessions, not even realizing she was blurring the homosexual image of our father that she had worked so hard to establish, that a month before their marriage she had gone to a hotel with Daddy because "he kept on and on at me." Perhaps I was ten at the time — I did not understand.

"Kiss your father good night," she said. "He's a good father to you children." But never kissed him on the mouth herself and only occasionally leaned over his chair and gave him a brief kiss on the forehead. I never felt any closeness between them except when they combined efforts to borrow money or ward off bill collectors. I grew up, for the first sixteen years of my life, knowing only this woman and this man, my sister and my grandfather Harry Goodenough. Everyone else existed only in an official capacity — teacher, doctor, saleslady — or in dreams.

The sight of my mother's body filled me with shame and deep disgust. She had large, heavy breasts, and her stomach, which stuck out when she took off her corsets, was covered with minute blue-white scars, very fine, like the lines on an ice-skating rink. She said they were stretch marks and happened when she was carrying me because I was too big. I could never imagine her young and running or in any way connected with the heroines of the romances she brought home from the lending library. She had a large white moon-shaped crater on her thigh — a small pox vaccination mark. I did not like to look at it — it was such a deadly white — in fact, I could not bear to think of her as having bodily sensations and functions at all. Blood spots on the back of her nightgown made me want to vomit, and she herself called menstruation by derogatory names: "the curse," "falling off the roof," "getting your grandmother." For three months after I began to menstruate I slept naked on the floor of my bedroom so as not to spot the sheets and let her know and spent my milk money stockpiling Kotex from the machines at school, taking the used ones back with me in my lunch kit to be disposed of in the girls' lavatory at recess. Later, because of course she eventually found out, we often ran out of sanitary pads and she would send my father out for them, not us, so that we wouldn't be "embarrassed." Parts of the body and bodily functions had nicknames as well. A vagina was a "tookie," a penis (although rarely mentioned) a "teakettle," a bowel movement a "grunter" or a "daily duty." It was all very coy and somehow dirty.

If someone broke wind my father said, "Somebody cut the cheese."

My mother said, "Pardon me, Mrs. Astor," and we all giggled self-consciously.

That men might embrace women was the stuff of fairy tales — I knew the truth. My erotic daydreams centred mostly on rescuing boys from cave-ins or burning buildings; rarely did I imagine myself kissing or being kissed.

At the same time I yearned over the bright and shining mothers in the *Journal* and *Woman's Home Companion*, slim-waisted, beautifully groomed (even in the kitchen) or out walking with their golden daughters in identical seersucker mother-daughter dresses.

Meanwhile I sat in the sitting room reading Nancy Drew.

"Mother."

"What?"

"*Please.*"

"What."

"Please put your shoes on."

Or gazed out the bedroom window at that other world where lovers walked the summer streets with their arms around one another's waists.

How could I believe that I would ever join them. It was impossible.

"Kiss your father good night. He's such a good father to you children."

five

Clara, because she had no one special in whom to confide, confided in everyone. Bank clerks, elevator operators, sales girls, encyclopedia salesmen. Wherever I went I felt I was thoroughly known and thoroughly discussed. "There goes the youngest Cleary girl. She's difficult, you know — very clever, but cold. It doesn't pay to be too clever, I always say. They're constantly in debt. Owe money all over town. The father's a spendthrift. Weak. Lily-livered. I don't know why she puts up with him." Everyone knew how our mother struggled to "keep their heads above water," how it "really got her down" sometimes, how she had "sacrificed everything for her girls." In my new boots, my new winter coat, my new plaid skirt and angora sweater, I walked the streets overwhelmed by my selfishness, the terrible burden of my mother's love.

"Where are you going, Isobel?"

"For a walk."

"Bundle up. You don't want a cold over Christmas."

It was snowing heavily, and I walked down Front Street and as far as the bridge, restless, unhappy, unable to break free. I longed for a friend, just one, but was too bitter and proud to make any friendly overtures myself. Somehow my mother always found out if we weren't invited to parties.

"Isn't Jeanette O'Connor having a sleigh ride tomorrow night?"

"I don't know. I guess so."

"I heard she was."

(How did she get her information? How?)

"Well, it's nothing to do with me."

"Don't you get on?"

"I don't know. I guess not. No."

"Why not? You're just as good as she is. They say her father's got a touch of the tarbrush anyway. Who does she think she is?"

"Could we drop it?"

"I'm just wondering why she didn't invite you, that's all. You used to be good friends."

"We were never good friends. Never."

"Well, it's all very strange. You're just as good as any of the rest of that bunch. Better."

"Maybe they don't think so."

"What?"

"I SAID MAYBE THEY DON'T THINK SO."

"There's no need to take that tone of voice with me. It's not my fault if you weren't invited, is it?"

She would go on and on until she reduced me to screams or tears. Each insult to me or Jane was a terrible insult to her. Much later I might hear her on the telephone, my heart beating painfully as I eavesdropped from the stairs.

"Hello. Is that Mrs. O'Connor? Jeanette's mother? Yes. Well, this is Clara Cleary, Isobel's mother. I know we shouldn't interfere in our daughter's lives, but I was wondering what caused the little spat between the girls? Isobel is quite broken-hearted that she wasn't invited to the sleigh ride.... What? Oh, I agree. Of course I wouldn't want you to speak to Jeanette about it. That's why I called now — I expect you to treat this as confidential.

It's just that Isobel is such a lonely, sensitive child — we have a difficult family life, you know — and perhaps she said something that hurt Jeanette's feelings without really knowing it. She has a sharp tongue, I know! ... You don't? No. Well. No harm in trying. You know how we mothers hate to see our children suffer, particularly if things can be ironed out.... You will? That's very good of you. I hope I didn't disturb you. No. Goodbye."

And I fled back up the stairs vowing silently, "Someday I'll kill you for that."

("I was only trying to help you."

"Stay out of my life."

"Don't talk to your mother like that."

"STAY OUT OF MY LIFE.")

The next day in school a sullen Jeanette gave me a reluctant invitation to her party.

"I'm sorry, I've got other plans."

"Oh? Too bad." She shrugged and walked away.

At recess I stayed inside to finish my Social Studies while the chosen girls stamped their feet and clapped their hands in the playground, discussing what they were going to wear that night.

When I came home from school my mother came out of the kitchen.

"Well?"

"Well what?"

"Did you and Jeanette make up your little quarrel?"

"I don't know what you're talking about."

"Did she invite you to the sleigh ride?"

"No. Of course not. I told you yesterday she hadn't."

I went upstairs, triumphant, and lay on the bed, shoving aside my wool slacks and pea jacket that my mother had laid out ready "just in case." After a while I got up and looked in the mirror. Was I really so ugly, so unpleasant? Why did no one like me? Why hadn't Jeanette invited me? What was the point of it all? It seemed to me not only that there was no justice in the world, there was no mercy. I pulled aside the curtain and looked out at the falling snow. If I went out in it and simply lay down somewhere — they said it didn't hurt to die that way.

Instead, of course, I went downstairs and ate my supper.
("Isobel, why do you look so sad?"
"It's nothing, Mrs. Carter. I have a headache."
"Would you like to go home?"
"No, thank you, I'm all right.")
Practising long faces in the mirror.

six

Isobel's family was always eating — we must have spent a fortune every year on food. There was roast beef or chicken every Sunday, roast potatoes, salad, bread and butter, usually two vegetables, pie or layer cake or pudding for dessert. Also (on Sunday) what my father called "relishes" — a plate of celery and radishes, green onions, pickles, pimento-stuffed olives. We were always told to "pass your plates," "eat up," "have some more milk." There was always white bread and butter on the table. When Jane rebelled, at about age thirteen, and refused to eat potatoes because she felt she was getting fat, my parents felt it was "unnatural," "unhealthy"; she would get anaemic. (And was forced to take One-a-Day brand vitamins with her breakfast.) On weekdays we did economize a little — codfish cakes, creamed chipped beef on toast, minute steaks or macaroni and cheese, but our father didn't really like these meals and often had a full dinner at school at lunchtime, as well as his dinner at home. He liked "good old-fashioned plain cooking" — that is to say, meat and potatoes — but he also liked lots of salt, pepper, Worcestershire sauce, preserves and butter. He went and bought our meat himself and was very particular that it be Grade A, would stand with two identical-looking rolled roasts in his hands, sniffing them and judging them by "feel," while the bloody-aproned butcher waited impatiently behind the counter. (He would pick up melons and sniff them, too, declaring he could tell when they were ripe.)

Sunday nights he made home-made soup from bones he'd got the butcher to throw in free, and we'd have soup and Philadelphia Cream Cheese sandwiches or cream-cheese-on-pear salad and cocoa from the tall rose-patterned chocolate pot, my only legacy from Grandma Cleary. (Jane got the cookie jar that matched it.) He would hum as he worked or sing one of his crazy songs.

> Oh the only girl I ever loved
> had a face like a horse and buggy.
> Be careful of that monkey wrench
> your father was a nut.

Slicing up carrots, chopping celery, adding a generous quantity of salt and pepper to the stock he had made very early in the day. "But the child ... was ... big ... ger than the fire ... man." Sometimes with one of mother's aprons on to protect his trousers. She would call, from upstairs, "How can you be hungry after that huge dinner?" But generally she'd come down too, when it was all ready, and nibble at some cream cheese and bread and butter. If not, she'd come to our rooms, where we were reading or, as we got older, studying and say, "You'd better go down. Your father does so much for you girls," and we would bring her up tea and toast on a chipped tray that advertised Coca-Cola.

Food was always offered after quarrels.

"Clara! Clara!" (Our father's voice from below.) "Aren't you gonna come down and eat some of this nice stew?" Sometimes he would bring it up and leave it outside her door. "I've got some nice lamb stew here for you, Muddie," lapsing into the name he often called her. "It's just outside the door."

But he was not back downstairs one minute before she flung open the door and picked up the tray, rushing downstairs, her eyes raw and red, her cheek pock-marked from the bedspread, flying into the dining room, where the two of us sat poking at our food — Daddy muttering it was "a damn shame" but mopping up his gravy with a piece of bread, like a rag — flinging the tray down on the table or sometimes throwing it at him — bits of vegetable and meat spraying everywhere.

"How *dare* you give me these great lumps of meat! How *dare* you!"

Bursting into tears, flying out again and up the stairs — the White Witch in her old nightgown. The key turned in the lock. We left our father, picking carrots off the rug, and said we weren't hungry any more. He would moon around downstairs for a while, cleaning up the disastrous meal, but also (as we were, upstairs, hearts thudding) waiting for the next attack.

Or sometimes she would come down and eat and maybe ask us to forgive her for "flying off the handle." Yet she, too, despite her warnings that our father's extravagance would land us all in the poorhouse (he said the same thing to her about the electricity, the quantities of clothes she bought for us, the dancing lessons), liked to have us "run down to the corner" for doughnuts or Oreo biscuits and ginger ale. And if we had a little Saturday or Sunday afternoon drive to Greene or Oswego she invariably suggested, if Daddy didn't get it in first, that we stop somewhere for a "treat." (But, in the autumn, when the schoolroom windows were decorated with construction paper Jack-o-Lanterns and witches, how lovely to drive out into the valley, near dusk, and buy a gallon jug of apple cider or little flat scalloped cakes of maple sugar from some country stand. And in the summer, remember the yellow squash, the beans, the corn, picked out by the roadside on the way up to or way down from Grandpa's Woods. There were good times too.)

There were Masonic picnics at State Park: the long trestle tables in the pavilion covered with Boston baked beans, macaroni and cheese, meat balls in gravy, potato salad, jellied salads, home-made rolls, chocolate fudge brownies. Over in the corner a man with a chef's hat was grilling hot dogs and hot dog buns. Ice cream sandwiches waiting in dry ice. Cokes or real lemonade or beer. My father loved these affairs although my mother (whose usual contribution, so far as I can remember, was a devil's-food cake) thought the women were "hoity-toity" in their crisp summer sheers and open-work sandals. Many were members of the Order of the Eastern Star and therefore knew one another very well. My father was very sad that she wouldn't join, that he had no son for De Molay, that we were not interested in the Rainbow Girls. Still, he steered us around and showed us off, often, to our embarrassment, breaking up little groups of men discussing golf scores or the latest headlines.

"Brother Brannon. Brother Wemple. I don't think you've met my daughters." We would stand there, shifting from one white sandal to the other while Daddy wedged himself into the conversation.

"Sure is a swell turn-out."

"Wish old Stan Johnson could be here to see it."

"Yeah. Say! Wasn't that a shame? Are you going to the funeral?"

Eventually one of us would tug his arm.

"Wha? Oh. Yeah. Better be gettin' along now."

Or we'd simply wander off, as out of place and ill at ease as Mother, who at least, by this time, had usually found *somebody* to tell her troubles to.

A man with a yellow rosette on his shirt approached us. "Hey, you two girls. "D'ya want to be in the three-legged race?"

We shook our heads and walked quicker, with more purpose. Nor in the relays or the potato race or the watermelon-eating contest. Sometimes Mother would give in and let us go swimming — warning us of course not to swallow any of the water and not to sit down on the toilet seats in the ladies' "because you never know."

We were shy, unused to changing rooms and so many people swimming. The lake was muddy unless you got way out and we were both indifferent swimmers. Mother would get up out of her chair (for of course she had followed us) and come down to the water's edge.

"Jane, Isobel. That's enough."

Boys raced one another, held each other's heads down and came up laughing and snorting, shouting feeble, show-off curses.

"All right, Miller. You're an asshole. Just wait till I catch up with you!"

Lovers, standing knee deep in the water, splashed and shrieked at one another. The lifeguard, bronze, arrogant, his hat pulled halfway over his eyes, blew his whistle from time to time. Fast girls in skimpy two-piece bathing suits ran after boys, shoving them, pushing them into the water. Screaming. Everyone laughed and shouted and was having a wonderful time.

A middle-aged man in a white rubber bathing cap did a superior Australian crawl, way out, out beyond the pleasure boats (fifty cents an hour), and people turned to look. I wished he had been my father.

"Isobel. Jane. Don't go any further out." Cupping her hands.

And once I put my hand down in the silty bottom and came up with a five-cent piece. I bought a pad of lined paper to write my poems on.

"Ha! What poems?"

"You don't know everything."

It was the only money I have ever found.

Later that night we would hear Daddy in the downstairs bathroom, cursing to himself and looking for the Sal Hepatica.

When Aunt Olive came to visit my father would go all out to "put on a good spread" and then would borrow money off her. She was short and plump, like her brother, but I liked her because she treated me like an intelligent human being and seemed to think we were "coming along all right." She wore rubber galoshes, had a Ph.D. in English and a wonderful folding umbrella. We would go down to the Greyhound bus station to pick her up.

"Ah. Warren. Good to see you." Kissing the air above our cheeks. "Isobel. Janie. How are you?" Daddy would grab her case and start away quickly — he didn't like the bus station or the second-rate-looking people sitting on the benches. Perverts or

Polacks or drunks being sick in the wastebasket. Cardboard suit-cases or cloth bundles piled up beside them.

"Warne!" Aunt Olive would call. "Warne!" She had a loud, husky and rather phlegmy voice. It usually turned out that she had checked another bag. Waving her stubs. "Warne!" My mother resented her, perhaps because she was a successful career woman, a university professor, but mostly I think because our father often turned to Aunt Olive to help "tide us over" in some crisis. And it was, after all, Aunt Olive's house. And at the same time was contemptuous, "an old maid," "a regular old fuss bud-get," "where did all her praying ever get *her*?" (For Aunt O. was also a devout Episcopalian, got up early on a Sunday morning, fasted, went to communion.) She always wore a good wool skirt, a twin set and a single string of pearls. Heavy walking shoes and opaque stockings. The colour of the twin sets varied; the skirt and shoes were usually brown. I liked her but viewed her with unease. I was supposed to be bright — did I really want to end up sack-shaped, on a Greyhound bus, honourary house mother to a group of sorority girls? Sometimes my mother would take on Aunt Olive and Daddy together, hint at dark, unnatural links between them.

"I don't want your filthy money. I don't owe you anything," then go upstairs and lock herself in until Aunt Olive took an earlier bus than planned.

"Goodbye. Take care of yourselves. Jane. Isobel." She gave a little "hem." There were tears in her eyes. "I hope your mother is feeling better soon."

They would go down the path together, Aunt O. rummaging in her handbag to be sure she had her ticket. Two short dumpy little figures, bewildered and helpless under the fury of his wife, her sister-in-law. Grandfather Cleary, stern-faced and with side whiskers, impeccably dressed, stared at us from his silver frame on the piano. Jane and I got out the cards and began to play "Crazy Eights."

Yet in some ways it was worse if we went up to Syracuse to visit her. Aunt O. would take us all out to a restaurant, her treat, and we squirmed with embarrassment as my father asked the waitress if the clam chowder was really fresh or how she would rate the Yankee pot roast. Mother usually said she wanted "something light — a breast of chicken, no potatoes, thank you," but when Aunt O. called back the waitress for the second time to change her order of succotash to garden peas: "No, maybe I'll leave it as it was. What do you think, Warren?" Mother would smile and say, "So long as you're here I think I *will* have potatoes after all." Then giggle in a very public way and say, "Aren't we *awful*." They usually had an extra basket of Parker House rolls and extra butter between them.

Jane: "What's Pêche Melba?"

Mother: "I don't know, dear. Where does it say it?"

"Here, under Desserts."

Daddy: "You want to stick to somethin' simple. Say, Olive, isn't this the place that's famous for its berry pies?"

"What?" (She was a little deaf.) "Oh. Yes. I believe the pies *are* very good. Are you going to have pie?"

Pie would be ordered and then changed to pie à la mode and then to strawberry shortcake while we squirmed in our seats with shame.

"Are you sure you use real cream, now? I don't want any of that ersatz stuff." And when it came, over her sherbet, Mother: "Just give me a little taste, Daddy, just to see what it's like."

("You didn't have to make such a pig of yourself."

"Who did?"

"You. You're digging your grave with your teeth, that's what you're doing."

"NNah. NNah. NNah."

But nothing could really faze him, not with a good meal behind him and a cheque she knew nothing about in his back pocket.)

However, Christmas was our high point, our epiphany of food and spending. The drawers would be crammed with papers marked, in red, *Final Notice*; the Dairyland man, turning his hat awkwardly as he spoke, would have been around twice — "If you could just let us have a little something on the bill"; the grocer had refused us any more credit. Mrs. Killam murmured, as

I curtsied to her in my new red velvet dress (we got our Christmas dresses early so that Cruchley could take our pictures, the annual surprise present for Harry), "Is your mother picking you up tonight, dear?" She would ask the same thing of Jane, in the seven-to-eight, to be sure I wasn't lying. "Is your mother picking you up tonight, dear?" I had had my hair permed the day before and was sure it smelled.

"No, ma'am. My father. He doesn't come in."

Yet somehow, incredibly, we managed. Switched grocery stores and meat markets, staved off the Dairyland man — "Just a little more time. You're a family man. You know how it is with kids at Christmas" — let the insurance lapse (again), made a quick call to Aunt Olive, did whatever was necessary to insure that this Christmas would be the merriest ever. Mysterious parcels were smuggled into the house by my mother. My father called "Don't come in!" if we knocked on his door to tell him supper was ready. We began to get cards, opened by my father and carefully counted.

"Don't get so many as I used to. First time in fifteen years we haven't had a card from Fred Watkins." These were put in a dented pewter bowl, one of our parents' few wedding presents which still survived, and sometimes stayed there for a whole year unless they were tossed in some already overfull drawer and forgotten. My father always wanted to get printed cards — "Warren and Clara Cleary and the girls" — but somehow restrained himself to boxes and boxes of Rustcraft or Hallmark Christmas scenes, preferably with a bit of glitter on them. (Harry had his own cards printed. A drawing or sometimes a photograph of Journey's End. They were large and had to go in special envelopes. One year there was a photograph of him, in lumber jacket and coonskin cap, shaking hands with Santa Claus on our snow-covered beach.) Jane and I wangled money for cards, too, and gave them out a few days early at school, hoping this would insure a good return. And money for matching wrapping paper and ribbon, matching cards. All this seemed very important at the time. When a crumpled brown-paper parcel arrived from my mother's brother, Uncle H.

(usually containing stocking caps or mittens), we felt insulted, at the same time we were pleased to have a package delivered through the mail, to think he had used thin dime-store wrapping paper and coloured string.

Daddy bought "old-fashioned" ribbon candy and sour balls, red, yellow, green, in glass jars, pralines, rock candy, Crosse and Blackwell tinned fig puddings, round boxes of glace fruits covered over with sunlight-coloured cellophane. Oblongs of store-bought fruit cake surrounded by corrugated red paper. Pounds of nuts and a new nutcracker because we couldn't usually find the old one. Tinned pumpkin, a box of icing sugar and extra butter for the hard sauce. The biggest turkey that would fit in our oven. A red net stocking full of goodies for the dog. It usually snowed, back then, for Christmas. We poured Karo syrup over the snow on the flat, back-porch roof, made honey-coloured patterns, then pulled it off and ate it. Soaked our feet in pans of lukewarm water if we stayed out too long. Heard, once again, our father's tale of how he went to lick a big icicle when he was a kid and got stuck to it, pulled the skin of his tongue right off. We made Christmas lists and I asked once again for a real Swiss music box.

We went out with our father and bought a big tree, not the "reasonable-sized" one we'd been sent for. But not the long-needled, delicate Scotch pine either. That was too expensive. We had to draw the line somewhere. Drove home with the trunk open, passing other cars with similar bushy behinds, as though we were all practising some ridiculous and inadequate disguise. Our chains cracked and whirred on the slippery streets.

Then a bucket of wet earth to set it up in and down from the attic a huge box full of odds and ends of ornaments — coloured balls which shattered into silver if you looked at them the wrong way, little mirrors to put behind the lights. Tinsel chains, tarnished but passable, strings of lights which had the misfortune to all go off at once if one bulb went. A faded red tissue-paper honeycomb bell to hang in the entrance to the sitting room. We added to this new tinfoil icicles and angel hair, Daddy warning us to "watch out," "go and put your slippers on," "watch

the dog, now, see she doesn't get any of that stuff up her nose."
Uneasy on the stepladder, Mother made to come and hold it
from below. Finally done, and the old star on top, a strange
thing, full of holes, that looked as though it had been inspired
by a colander, but lovely once a light was stuck in it (Daddy
anxious here, too, rubbing his palms on his trousers, careful not
to get electrocuted). We spread out a sheet and brought down
our presents to the family as well as the few parcels that had
arrived from relatives. Jane turned out the lights and pulled
back the front room curtains so the tree would show. Daddy suggested we have some cocoa and a little slice of that fruit cake,
right now. Jane and I brought ours into the sitting room to be
near the tree. We sang Christmas carols together, or listened to
Lionel Barrymore on the radio. Mother went out in the kitchen
and singed the pin feathers off the turkey — a smell of burning
hair drifted out to us. But not unpleasant. Part of Christmas. I
wished I were a Catholic so that I could go to midnight Mass
and feel Christ born on my tongue. Daddy put out slices of stale
bread to dry, even more, overnight. Then we were sent upstairs
and right to sleep while Mother's steps went up and down up
and down carrying presents from her bedroom cupboard to the
dining room table, where she and our father would finish wrapping them.

And in the morning such a wealth of presents — nearly
everything we'd asked for. Daddy played Santa and handed
them out.

"Let's see. To Isobel from Santa. What could that be?"

"Find one for me, Daddy. Find one for Mother."

We always got clothes. Velveteen dresses and dainty blouses,
seen in November and held on layaway until Mother picked
them up. Cologne, petticoats, black ballerina skirts, Capezio
shoes, angora sweaters (which we kept in the icebox because we
were told that that would make them even silkier), figure skates,
real bunny-fur ear muffs and mittens, Columbia bicycles identical except for colour, whatever it was that this year we simply
had to have. Earlier, dolls' houses (two), dolls, doll clothes, doll-
house furniture, blocks, a kindergarten set. Only once, a book,

when I was ten, *Great Expectations*, because I asked for it. New party shoes already worn to the dancing class Christmas party but wrapped back up and set out under the tree.

We gave Mother her silver-plated bonbon dish or set of Friendship Garden toiletries, Daddy his Hickock belt or Zippo lighter. They gave each other ties, socks, stockings, a new night-gown, a frying pan, a waffle iron, a new fishing rod, all picked out by themselves and then given to the other one to wrap up.

Once, when we were very small and living in Ithaca, our father had presumed to buy a matched set of dressing table accessories — hand mirror, brush, comb, in a splendid presenta-tion case. I remember the backs of the articles because they had lovely blue fake cloisonné work on them with a tiny basket of roses in the very centre. There was a terrible fight about that and he had to take it back to the store. We were passing one knife around the table at the time because all the handles of the others had come unstuck and we had no money or energy to fix them. Maybe she was right.

At around one o'clock Harry came, usually without the housekeeper, who was given a few days off. He would look at the mounds of presents displayed in their boxes under the tree, smile sardonically and say nothing. He gave us our money in special Christmas folders he got at the bank; Mother got a check for twenty-five. I can't remember if he ever gave Daddy anything except the yearly renewal to the *National Geographic*. The announcement card, shaped like a tiny version of the mag-azine, was always hung on the tree. We gave him his new studio photograph of us, a cardigan, whatever we had made for our class project. The turkey, which my father had put on at day-break, stuffing it himself with his own recipe for sage/apple/onion dressing, sent out its tempting aroma, tempting even in spite of the candy canes we'd sucked, the tangerines, the nigger toes, the hardy candy at the bottom of our stockings. Harry sat in the best chair and we "entertained him" (which usually meant showing him every last bit of loot, trying things on, making him feel this or smell that. Once in a while he would say, "Your dad must've come into a gold mine" or "Didn't Santa go anywhere else but here?" but we would smile uneasily and he'd fall silent again).

Jane and I had already set the table, dished out the cranberry sauce into our only jelly dish, put out a big dish of "relishes," made a centrepiece from leftover greens and the novelty candles we collected. We had new water glasses to replace the ones we'd broken during the year. The best china, bought during the bonanza of my grandmother Cleary's estate.

Harry sat at one end of the table, Daddy at the other. We had mounds of yams or sweet potatoes, ordinary mashed potatoes, brussels sprouts, squash, a jam jar full of giblet gravy because we didn't have a gravy boat. Cranberry sauce. White meat. Dark meat. Daddy, slyly: "Pass your plate up here, Mr. Goodenough, for a little more of the breast." Jane and I, slightly tipsy on the once-a-year wine in the fruit cup, kicked each other and giggled. Harry raised his eyebrows in mock astonishment.

"Da goo turkee," said my father, his mouth full. "Beth we evah ha."

"Warren... Warne!"

"Wha?"

"You've got a piece of brussels sprout caught on your front tooth. Take it off. It's revolting." (Helping herself to a little more gravy and mashed potatoes.)

"What would you like, Dad?"

"Nothing thanks. I've done very well."

"You sure you won't have a bit more of this turkey, sir?"

"Not for me, thank you. You have some."

"Don't mind if I do. Went to a new place this year — Perroni's. You ought to try it." Then: "Clara, is there any more of them sprouts?"

Fig pudding for dessert. Mince or pumpkin pie. ("How about a bit of cheese to go with that pie?") Ice cream for those who wanted it.

Under the table the dog chewed noisily on her special rubber bone.

I don't remember that we ever had any conversation, except about the weather, or Aunt Hettie, who lived in Connecticut, or Uncle H. Perhaps, I thought bleakly, this is all that anyone has. Jane passed round the coffee and the after-dinner mints. We stacked the dishes by the kitchen sink. Daddy came out to dig the stuffing from the turkey so we wouldn't all die of ptomaine poisoning. Then he retired to the sitting room and promptly fell asleep. Harry said he'd have to be getting home.

"Oh, *Dad*. Already? Let me wrap you up a bit of turkey and some pie."

"No thanks. I'll have my usual milk toast tonight. Nothing much tomorrow after a feed like that. Mrs. Veal left some stuff in the refrigerator.

"Did you walk up? Warren'll drive you back. He doesn't mind."

He gave her a gesture of dismissal and put on his scarf and gloves.

"Let him sleep. I need the walk." Mother would put all his presents in a paper bag and sneak in a piece of pie or parcel of turkey at the bottom. He probably never ate them.

As I got older I used to walk him halfway home, feeling hot and overfed and inexplicably out of sorts. Once he stopped me under a street light — we had said nothing since leaving the house, the snow creaking like stiff leather under our galoshes.

"Isobel."

"What?"

He tilted my chin up to the light, still a tall man. Still a handsome man. I was afraid of him — I knew he judged us in his heart — but I loved him terribly. He shook his head and let me go.

"What is it?"

"Nothing. I'm an old man. You turn back here."

"Is something the matter, Grandpa?"

"Nothing I can fix." He crossed the street and melted into the falling snow.

But the worst Christmas of all was the year she tore the ornaments off the Christmas tree that night (Why did she do it, Isobel? I can't remember), crushed them under her heel, scattered the turkey carcass, wrenching it apart, outside in the backyard in the darkness.

"This is what I think of your Christmas! This is what I think of your goddamn Merry Christmas." Smashing a coffee cup against the kitchen wall.

"What's the matter with you now?"

"No! You wouldn't know, would you? Or those two spoiled brats of yours. I work" (smash) "and I slave" (smash) "and nobody so much as raises a finger to help me."

"All right, Mother. Mother, we'll do the dishes." Begging, weeping, the tree in the sitting room tilted drunkenly for all the passers-by to see. "Stop it, please stop it."

"Why? Why should I? I'm not going to take any more orders from you two when I never get any thanks from you or your no-good father." Smash.

It was no use. We rushed upstairs, howling, creatures primitive and utterly heart-broken, past the stricken tree, our father outside in the dark, weeping, trying to find the bits of turkey with a flashlight, blubbering, "My God, my God, my God."

The neighbourhood cats advanced.

Such were the feasts of my childhood, of Isobel's youth.

"Isobel, do you remember when she smashed the bathroom mirror with a cold-cream jar?"

"No."

"Of course you do. The frame hung there for days and one night, brushing your teeth, you chanced to look up and saw only a blank piece of cardboard and not your face. Your face had disappeared."

"I remember. I thought it was an omen at the time."

seven

Ah, but there was always Harry! Mythical at the top of the stairs in the lantern light. How I loved him, how I envied him his wealth, his wisdom, his bottom drawer of superfluous unworn shirts, his magical roll of dollar bills, his lack of fear. The fact that he was head of a whole department.

And was myself afraid of his contempt.

("Bring the axe down hard, Isobel."

"Harry, I can't. I'm afraid I'll cut my foot off."

"Goddamnit, bring the axe down hard!"

The hired man, leaning against the porch steps, rolling a cig-arette and licking the paper with one sweep of his tongue. Watching me. Grinning at my cowardice. He always had at least one blackened thumbnail.

"You want me to go down and tinker with that motor, Mr. Goodenough?"

I wore fear like a hump on my back.)

Harry — shrunken a little in the city, perhaps, but ever the bearer of presents and a certain solidarity. Bringer of our first (and only) puppy, and not just handing it to us, his choice, but driving up one Saturday in the old Lasalle and saying curtly, "Hop in." Off for a secret ride in the country to a farmhouse where I remember a calendar advertising fertilizer — the girl in the picture was dressed in a red satin cowboy shirt and white ten-gallon hat; her breasts lolled invitingly against the fence. We were shown into a back room where there was a mother spaniel and four puppies on an old quilt.

"Choose one," he said. And then, "You'd better make sure it's a female. Your mother wouldn't want a male." The farm kids standing sullen in their rubber boots — they didn't want the pups to go.

We chose the runt, both of us at the same time, and sat up all night with a hot-water bottle wrapped in flannel and an alarm clock, keeping the miserable, whimpering flea-ridden animal company. When she was six months old we had her spayed so that she wouldn't have babies.

("Did it hurt her?"

"Of course not, Isobel. The doctor gave her something to make her sleep."

I couldn't bear to look at the pink exposed strip of belly with its little track of stitches. When she came to me for petting I pushed her away in disgust.)

Bringer of the annual socks of pennies. Two white rabbits once who subsequently died and were taken out with the garbage. Sender of a yard of candy through the mail — that's what the box said — "a yard of candy for you" — when he took a rail trip out to the Rockies and out beyond to British Columbia, Canada, and the Empress Hotel (where else could such a grandfather stay?), then down to California and Hollywood and back across the States. Pullmans (of course) all the way. (Aunt Olive did the same thing on a bus, years later. We weren't, but should have been, impressed.) We fought over who would get the candies wrapped in foil.

Who came up one night and put signs on the front of our house — BEWARE OF THE DOG — so that neither the milk nor the morning paper was delivered and we couldn't understand why. Or came to the back door in long grey whiskers and skull cap, in an old black overcoat and false nose, begging our Mother for a cup of milk and some bread. (Which she gave and was pouring boiling water over the cup when he came round to the front, still dressed in the old overcoat and cap but minus the whiskers and false nose, and rang the bell again.)

Once, when we were having Sunday night supper with him, he opened the drawers of his bureau and showed us shirt after gleaming shirt, still folded and pinned as it was in the store, pairs of socks, thin boxes containing ties, leather wallets, cuff links. All presents; all never used. But Harry wore the cardigan we gave him, sometimes put on the beautiful dark-blue smoking jacket, displayed our drawings and our tipsy ceramic ash trays. Loved us. ("Did he, Isobel?" "He did.")

And once he devised a marvellous map, aged it with heat and spots of candle wax, indicated buried treasure on the beach. We ran from clue to clue (old stumps, the flagpole, a disused hornet's nest, the outhouse), laughing, knowing it was all a fake. But finally measuring off twenty paces from the property stake, fifteen degrees from the last pine tree below the cottage. We dug and dug and knew there would be a note with a message "Ha. Ha. Long John Silver." Then Jane hit something metallic with her spade. We knelt and dug with our hands. A tin box, heavy. We had to run and get a file to pry it open. A thousand brand new pennies winked at us in the light from the setting sun.

A cookie jar shaped like a pig that he wired one day and attached to a small burglar alarm.

Trips to Ross Park Zoo in the wintertime, a small bag of round pink-and-white striped candies for the animals, a small bag for ourselves. He took us to all the Hope and Crosby "Road" shows.

Mother said, "Dad do you really think they're suitable?" Walking home, one on each side of him, in the dark, over the Court Street Bridge. The Pin-up Girls of H.B. Goodenough.

For all this we were willing to play his games, call him Uncle Harry when he took us for Saturday lunch at the Ritz Tea Room. Watch him kid with Lilian, the hostess, who wore her blonde hair in a high pompadour and looked, in her smart dress and corsage, like a lady in an advertisement. Maybe we knew all along it was only kidding, a harmless sop to his ego in a society which would call a man "an old fool" or "oversexed" (terms our mother used about him sometimes) if he still felt desire at seventy-five. And his had been a "love match" — we had heard the story from Mother. How young Harry Goodenough, without a penny to his name, struggling to get through the polytechnic, had seen an even younger girl sitting on her porch swing. Marched up the stairs and rang the bell, announcing to her surprised mother, my great-grandma, "In six years' time that's the girl I want to marry" and kept his word. (But killed her in the end.)

("Harry, what d'you call this tree?"

"It doesn't matter."

"It does. It does. What d'you call it, Harry?"

"Why don't you name it yourself? Why take a name that someone else has given it?"

"Because that's its real name."

"No, Isobel. It's not."

"What's its real name, then?"

"God knows. I don't."

"Is my real name not Isobel?"

"It might be. Wait and see.")

We went down to the creek in our rubber boots and dug up clay from the creek bed. A frog surveyed us from a lily pad. Our father was scaling fish out behind the boathouse. I could hear the rasping sound of his fish knife. Scritch. Scritch. Scritch.

"Be careful. There's quicksand there."

"Who says?"

"Daddy said so."

"He's a goddamn fool."

Certainly he never hired his housekeepers for their beauty — except perhaps Mae-Love Woolcock, who stayed with him longer than any of the others. Who stayed until Aunt Hettie came and kicked her out. They were all widows or "grass widows," as our mother called them, all near or into middle age.

I suspect, knowing him, he may have hired them for their names. Besides Mae-Love, I remember Vera Veal, Virginia Ball, Gertrude Piano and Bertha Bush. Harry had a picture taken of Mrs. Bush (a tiny, worried little woman who taught us how to tat on rainy days and had been companion to a very old lady before she answered our Harry's ad) in his coonskin cap and with a (never used) rifle in her hands. Underneath he had printed "DANGEROUS BERTHA" and she loved it. Gertrude Piano believed in ESP, and Jane and I persuaded her to try our Ouija Board with us, moving the little heart-shaped part around until it spelled, drunkenly, "S — O — O — N" when we asked, against Mrs. Piano's feeble protests, whether she would ever marry again. But she was rather old and always put her feet up after lunch because her ankles swelled. I think even she knew the Ouija Board was joking.

Virginia Ball took us into the village for some milk and, on the way back, stopped at Adams' Dance Hall for a glass of beer. We were intrigued and astounded by this, particularly as we knew our mother, and probably our grandfather, would never approve. We sat at a table on the verandah and looked with interest at the coloured lights strung along the roof. It was a weekday afternoon and there was nobody there but us and old Roy Adams, who served Virginia her beer and had helped our grandfather build his camp. At one time he and his brother had owned nearly the whole lake — Harry had bought from them. Roy had two fingers missing from one hand and was partially paralyzed by a stroke so that he walked as though he were carrying an invisible but very heavy pail. He didn't attempt to make any conversation with us — just went back inside, letting the screen door slam behind him. Virginia gave me a little sip of her beer.

"Bleah. It tastes terrible."

"Honey, you mean it tastes terrible to *you*."

She never invited us to go again. Whether old Roy recognized us and from some sense of gratitude or old times' sake or something got in touch with Harry or whether Virginia actually did something else which angered him I don't know. Anyway, she left a couple of weeks later. Harry, more stern than I had ever seen him, drove her down to Utica to get the bus. Mother (secretly glad, I'm sure) offered to housekeep until we all went back to town.

A few days later, when we were all asleep, there was a terrific banging at the back door. Very frightening. Jane and I clutched each other tight, convinced it was, at last, Floyd Masters, the ever-wanted outlaw with maroon eyes. Or a murderer, fleeing from Ontario — hungry, desperate, a man who would stop at nothing, Mother hissed at Daddy, beyond the faded curtain.

"Warren! Warne!"

"Wha...?"

"Somebody's banging at the back door."

"Jesus." I could almost hear his heart pounding.

"Go and find out what's going on."

"No sir. I'm not goin' out there in the dark. Let him bang. Jesus. D'you think I'm crazy?"

Mother fumbled for her slippers.

"I should have known *you* wouldn't go. It might be somebody hurt." (But we could tell she didn't think so.)

"Mother, don't go!"

She hissed back at us "Shh. Stay where you are. Go back to sleep." As if we could!

I prayed that Harry had remembered to lock the screen door. It was overcast. There was no moon. (Please, God, I'll never be bad again, just don't let anybody kill us.)

Mother doing something in the big room, then her steps across the kitchen floor, the back door flung open.

(Please, God, I promise you.)

"Stop it," whispered Jane, "you're hurting me." Daddy was sitting on the edge of his cot, smoking his last cigarette.)

Mother's high, thin, angry voice. "What do you want? What do you mean by this?"

A man's indistinct murmur ("There, what did I tell you?" Daddy whispering, "Jesus Christ, oh Jesus."), then, oh miracle, steps going uncertainly back down the steps.

"And don't come moseying around this place again!"

We rushed out just as Harry, rubbing his eyes and very cross, came out from the other side of the house.

"What the hell!"

Mother stood in the kitchen, a lumber jacket over her night-gown, hair straggling down her back. She had snatched up one of the two rifles that hung over the fireplace. Stood there now flushed and triumphant, the rifle in her hands, like an illustration of Tugboat Annie in the *Saturday Evening Post*.

"Some drunken bum asking for Virginia."

"WHAT?"

"Some drunken bum. I've never seen him before. 'Wan Ginny,' he said. 'Where's Ginny?' But I showed him what's what!"

Harry looked from our mother to us, still shaking and now with cold as well as shock, to our father, who had come out no farther than the door that led to the main room. Then he began to laugh.

"Clara, did you really threaten that fellow with that gun?"

"I certainly did." Proud, rosy-cheeked, she stood tall. Defender of her brood. I saw her in a new and favourable light.

"Give it here, carefully." He shook the shells on the table. "Did you know it was loaded?"

"No. I ..." She sat down.

"You might really have blasted him."

Mother turned pale. "You had that loaded gun up there where the children could have got at it any time!"

"Sure. For just such an emergency. But I never thought any-body'd touch it but me. The other one's loaded, too," he said.

Mother made him empty out the other right then, and he did so, still chuckling to himself.

We all had some cocoa and then went back to bed. But what if Mama ...? I couldn't sleep.

Harry drove into the village next day, but he never did find out who it was. Mother's description wasn't very definite. A dark-haired man, in a mackinaw, drunk. Still, he let it be known the rifle had been loaded and nobody ever troubled us that way again. All in all, that was a pretty successful summer for our mother.

"Where were you, Warren?" asked Harry the next morning at breakfast.

Daddy just grinned sheepishly and forked another load of pancakes into his mouth. Mother was sitting in the house-keeper's seat.

"What would you like for dinner, Dad?" she said, pouring herself another cup of coffee.

"Whatever you like," he said, "whatever you like."

Harry had a knife that collapsed when you tried to cut with it, a tin that said "Peanut Brittle" but when you unscrewed the lid two huge green snakes — cloth-covered springs — flew up in your face, a book called *Gone With the Wind* that had been hollowed out inside and contained a little pan with beans glued on, a box with a picture of two lovers silhouetted under a harvest moon: "A Hammock Built for Two." (And inside a tiny pink brassiere stuffed with cotton wool.) One year he found a pretty cardboard lady sitting on a chair and offering a plate of cookies in a shop window somewhere. He bought her and sometimes would sit her in Ga-Ga's old rocking chair and he'd sit facing her. "Best woman I ever had."

Possessed a collection of marvellous hats (ten-gallon, coon-skin, old metal fireman's hat, an opera hat which came up tall, whoosh, if you shook it right). A Pablum box full of arrowheads.

And was really an ascetic in his habits — little food, no tobacco, no alcohol. Taught us to make soap from wood ashes and how to fold the flag the way it was supposed to be folded. Helped me make up new Burma Shave signs on rainy days.

> Be Careful Now
> And Don't Get Funny
> Remember Birds
> These Signs Cost Money
> Burma Shave

Unclenched my hands one day and said, "Nothing in life is worth clenching your hands about."

Walked spry and sure-footed across the roof to repair a hole in the asphalt. Let me sit on his lap and cuddle him.

We had Harry and Harry was lord of the lake and sky, still laughed when I called it "Grandpa's Woods." Gave me a wooden puzzle with a shiny dime embedded in one piece. (I never solved it.) Chased us around the big table after he had lathered his face, ready to shave with his beautiful, villainous, bone-handled razor. "Won't you give the old man a kiss?" Giggling and squeaking like mice.

Yet once, sitting at the table, when I couldn't tell him how to identify poison sumac, I looked him straight in the eye and said, "Well, at least I know what 'fuck' means."

It was Harry who insisted I have my mouth washed out with soap. But made fish come raining from a little airplane in the sky. Said one day to our mother: "Don't fuss over them. Let them grow."

Was rich, while we were poor; handsome, while we were plain; loved by all, while we were loved by none. Could take clocks apart and put them back together.

But lonely?

("They said you looked like him. They said you had his eyes.")

eight

4:17

"Isobel," said my grandfather, "run up to the Daleys' and find out what that goddamned racket is all about." And that's how we discovered the war in the Pacific was over. It had meant little to us, this war. Just after the attack on Pearl Harbour our father, overweight, over forty, had gone down to the local draft board to see if he could enlist but was rejected — much to his relief, I'm sure. He had been a bugler in World War I, joined very near the end and never got farther than a training camp in New Jersey, where he picked up some mysterious bladder infection and came home. I have seen a picture of him, very shy and slim in his uniform, bugle under his arm, standing in front of a pup tent. That boy was just as unreal to me as the young girl Sharon Cleary or Clara Goodenough in her cloche standing by a Stutz Bear Cat that belonged to her friends. My father looked like a young and very reluctant Canadian Mountie.

Harry was much too old to go. We had no big brothers, and the closest relative I knew about was a very remote cousin, a second or third cousin of my mother's whose middle name was Jesus. He was somehow connected with old Aunt Deveena out at Goodenough, and I saw a picture of him once when we went to visit the cemetery.

There were posters, of course, everywhere. On the wall above the counter in the meat market: "A slip of the Lip May Sink a Ship"; at the D.L. and W. Railway Station: "Uncle Sam Needs You!" and "Loose Talk Costs Lives." Or the one that frightened me the most of all, on billboards, "Shh! The Enemy Might Be Listening," with grotesque caricatures of the Axis leaders. Grocery stores, department stores and banks, always places where one could be stopped and challenged or humiliated, took on an even more sinister cast with those posters plastered on the walls.

There were little silk flags in front-room windows as we walked downtown or over to Harry's house, mostly blue stars but occasionally a gold. Kate Smith sang "Buy a Bond Today" as well as "God/ Bless/ A/mer/ee/ka," and the downstate aunts sent us rows of bright green twenty-five cent savings stamps to put toward our Liberty Bonds. There were a few Victory Gardens at the foot of Johnson Avenue, and we took our old wagon around collecting fat in tins which we turned in for ten cent savings stamps at school. Names were added to the Honour Roll at the First Presbyterian Church, and Harry put up a sticker on the back of the outhouse: "Is This Trip Necessary?" There was the occasional air raid drill where Jane and I sat together on Mother's bed, in the darkness, behind drawn window shades, but we had done this when bill collectors came and that was more real, more frightening, than the remote possibility of an enemy attack.

We tried Instant Postum and Mother kneaded bright orange-coloured pellets into the dead-white margarine so that it would look like butter, only it never did and our father would never eat it — "None of that fake stuff for me." Jane and I saved cellophane and tinfoil and the inside tops of Ovaltine tins, which we had used to exchange for Captain Midnight badges or secret code rings, were replaced by cardboard. The boys and girls in the ads for Colgate dental creme, Vaseline hair tonic, Wildroot creme oil and the like all wore uniforms now, and one Christmas we each chose a uniformed WAVE doll, with real hair, as our "special" present.

Jews were made into bars of soap or lamp shades; babies were bayonetted, roasted and eaten like spring chickens. But all this was less real than the creaks on the stair or my own nightmares about giants. Once a boy at school showed me a blurry photograph of a pile of Japanese ears — it didn't disgust me, nor surprise. Adults were quite capable of doing such things. The day before my father had threatened my mother with the cleaver. Or so she said. There was a scream and she called to us, "Come down here, come down here right now." In the kitchen the green-handled cleaver lay on the floor. My father's face was wet — she had thrown a glass of water over him. I stood there, shaking, unwilling to believe, hating them both for waking me out of my sleep. And then we were to choose. Which one to stay with. Neither. ("Harry.") We knew better than to answer.

And *he*, trying to impress me with his stupid photograph of ears!

Because of my love of words and my mother's particular obsessions, I mistakenly associated Germany with germs. Unclean. You could hear it. Their language was full of spit and phlegm. They had used mustard gas in the last war, why not germs in this one? A test tube full could wipe out a continent. But the woman in the German bakery on the corner of Walnut Street? My father, who had taken a year of German, liked to go there and speak to her. She had rosy cheeks and a spotless white apron. She gave me broken buttermilk or molasses cookies, but I never ate them once I understood about the germs. I took them home and flushed them down the toilet. Daddy said she was a good American, but in California the Japanese Americans were being put in concentration camps. Why not the Germans? Wasn't she part of the collective guilt? And Mother said the Jews probably deserved everything they got. The Italians? What could you expect from a Catholic country?

But I wished I had a big brother to write to on V-mail or a flag to hang in our front room window. Even a dead big brother would do. Someone who had helped to sink an Axis sub or bring down a Jap Zero. It was all very well to talk about the Man Behind the Gun. Staying at home was only the coward's way out.

And we got a new girl in second grade. Her name was Heather Martin and she was English. Her sister Margaret was in grade five. They had been evacuated from Britain and were being looked after by one of the richest families in town. Heather wore a wristwatch with a real leather strap, had beautiful rosy cheeks and wavy hair. Within a week she was first choice for Bat Ball and invited to two birthday parties. I envied and hated her. The Lewises had a private tennis court and a beautiful house on The Heights. Heather was going to get a horse. Once, when she suddenly put her head down on her desk and wept, the teacher told us quietly and yet very dramatically just to get on with our workbooks, Heather was probably thinking about the war. Two other little girls began to cry in sympathy, but I sat there with a heart like stone. Why should she, who had been on a ship across the ocean, had experienced the excitement of the Blitz, had seen the King of England at his balcony, waving, with the Queen and Princess Elizabeth and Margaret Rose, why should she have any *sympathy*? And now she had a wristwatch and was going to have a horse. I would cheerfully have given up both my parents for that. Poor Heather my ass.

For weeks I went around hoping, praying, that I was adopted. That my real parents, preferably English and absolutely wealthy, would send a telegram and claim me: MISSING HEIRESS FOUND AT LAST. ELECTS TO RETURN TO WAR-TORN HOMELAND.

I would continue to write to Harry, of course, and come over every summer to Journey's End. I might even, after the war, bring my horse over too. His name was Stormy Rex.

Meanwhile I sat at the dinner table and said cooly, "Pass the butter, Mother, if you are my mother. Pass the salt, Daddy, if you are my daddy."

The downstate aunties sent us sterling-silver identification tags on thin silver chains. "Isobel M. Cleary," in beautiful copperplate script. Did they really think we were going to be bombed and blasted? That Jane or I would be found crying amidst a pile of rubble? Possibly so. They were very old and very conservative. I wore my tag with mixed feelings. I loved the silver and the script (my own handwriting was terrible and my sentences were never tacked up on the bulletin board) but I did not like to be so absolutely *chained* to me. If a bombing did occur, which I doubted, I had every intention of running away. Had already hidden in my room two packages of Vita-Sert and some Band-aids. ("But where would you have run to, Isobel? You who would not even cross over the bridge alone?")

So much longing to escape, so much hoping to be rescued. Parents do not think it is possible in a child of six to ten. How incredibly wrong they are. At six I already understood, although I could not have articulated it, that Jane and I were the dream images projected above the wasteland of our mother's life. We both realized — for hadn't we been told over and over? — that our parents stayed together only for our sakes — that our father was a "Mama's boy," most probably a "pervert" (although we didn't know what that meant) and not a "good provider." In other words, a failure. "Even the United States Army won't have him."

She sat on our beds in her old satin nightgown and told us wonderful tales of her youth: of a pony and trap and the local girls who used to come in and help Ga-Ga with the housework, of a beloved Boston bull terrier they called "Precious Pads." Of places with incredible names like Shinhopple or Raquette Lake; of how Harry had come to New York, one Thanksgiving, when she was studying there and had seen a huge turkey in the window of a smart restaurant, gone in and bought it, "just like that," and brought it to her and her friends who lived in a rather arty woman's residential hotel.

Of how she had left New York and a fine future to nurse your Aunt Hettie back to health — after she broke down and drank iodine, stood on a window ledge eight floors up screaming she was going to jump, jump, jump, was saved, collapsed and sent to Bellevue.

Of the time she (my mother) slept for three days without stopping and missed her exams because she did housework for some people in Brooklyn in exchange for room and board and was just too exhausted to wake up. The doctor said, "Let the poor girl sleep."

And about a man named Julian who was a patron of the arts and had a daughter who became a famous violinist. A bit of a "stage-door Johnny" but very "gone" on her and on Mary Martin too, maybe, and so perhaps it was just as well. And something about bathtub gin and somebody getting her silly at the railway station in Hoboken so that she dropped her purse and everything rolled out. After that she vowed she would never.

A pervert had something to do with lavatories and handkerchiefs. We were all she had left.

I would select a tune and shove it into my head: "Mairsie Doats and Doasie Doats and Little Lambsie Divy" or, later, "Dance, Ballerina, Dance" or a tune from *South Pacific*. At the same time I willed her to go away go away go away, to stop the endless flow of a past which threatened to rise up and drown us all.

When I didn't get the part of the Red Red Robin in the Brownie play she made a big fuss. I was just a daffodil, with all the others. But I liked my green and yellow crêpe-paper costume, my new green socks. "You're just as good as Winkie Wainwright — it's only because her mother's in the Junior League." She fought our battles for us, always, and then turned on us, weeping, "What have I done to deserve such daughters? Look in the mirror, Isobel, look at your face."

Indignities and feuds stretching back to the eighteenth century. Old leather-covered photograph albums dragged out and the lights turned on — we blinked painfully. "Here. This is your great-uncle Jesse. A fine one he was — never came to your grandfather's aid when he should have." Blah blah blah blah blah. She had dress boxes and candy boxes full of photographs and photo albums. One of these days she was going to ... Many photographs of us as babies. Everyone said "How beautiful" — we had been perfect; everyone said why don't you put them in for modelling? Could a swan become a duckling?

Aunt Olive was caught with some girls in the Ross Park Cemetery — Grandpa Cleary took a horse whip to her and that's why. Unhealthy (the Clearys), unnatural. And the Goodenoughs cold and proud.

In her worst tirades: "Your precious Harry." "Your precious father." "You and your sister in your glad rags," Terrible. The words burned into us like acid. To come from such tainted stock! My father — contemptible — a pervert. My sister and myself — parasites, monsters, demanding clothes, money, expensive presents, while she, Clara, mended her stockings and went without.

At first, when we were quite young, we would rush out and beat on our mother's locked door, crying, "We're sorry, sorry, sorry." And hear the terrible thick voice inside shouting, "Go away. It's too late. Go away." Later, much later, there were letters, not talks — hurled into our rooms like time bombs or grenades, and then the click of her locked door.

The next day she would ask to be forgiven. On the weekend we would all go downtown and she would pick out dresses for us to try on at Wiggins, Pollard and Baines or MacLeod's. My father would sit on a chair brought out by some contemptuous saleslady and Mother would bring us forth for a "fashion show."

"Sure," he would say, uncomfortable in his old suit, his frayed cuffs. "Swell. That looks just swell." The fitter would be called in and the dresses would be taken up or in and then sent to Layaway, to be called for later. We went to the Home Dairy for lunch and then back to our dreary house.

We were enrolled in Mrs. Killam's dancing classes and Mother had our pictures taken at Cruchley's one more time. When the proofs came she said he didn't do us justice any more. (Harry had a little leather case she gave him. Inside were two photographs of my sister and myself, aged five and six, in green velveteen dresses, little poke bonnets and velvet muffs. They were hand-coloured by Mr. Cruchley's assistant, Rose. On the cover it said "The Pin-up Girls of H.B. Goodenough." Stamped in gold. He took it with him everywhere.)

The *Press* published lists of our boys who were killed or missing in action. I curtsied to Mrs. Killam, when it was my turn, and prayed she wouldn't ask to see my mother after class. I wore white gloves and patent-leather shoes. I learned to do the waltz ("*One*, two, three, *one*, two, three, *one*, two, three"), the Fox Trot ("Step together, Step together, slide, slide"), the rhumba and the tango. When it was boys' choice I usually danced with another girl.

My parents' angry voices came up through the hot-air register. My mother left us, got as far as Scranton, Pennsylvania, and returned. One night she smashed all the glass in all the frames of the countless family photographs on the old upright piano.

"That's what I think of your precious family. *That's* what I think of you all."

In school we learned to conjugate the verb "to be."

> Be
> Is
> Are
> Was
> Were
> Am
> Being
> Been

I wanted to walk across the room and step on all the glass splinters — anything instead of this terrible coldness — but remained, instead, at the edge of the room, transfixed by the sight of my father weeping.

I hid aspirins under my pillow and prayed that she would find them, collected all my father's rusty razor blades and put them underneath my socks.

("Isobel, what are you doing with those razor blades in your drawer?"

"I want them to sharpen pencils. I'm taking them to school."

94

"I don't believe you."

"It's true. Teacher asked us to bring them. The pencil sharpener's broken."

Looking her in the eye. Coldly. Daring her to suspect. Wanting to make her sorry.

"Well, take them away tomorrow. I'll give you a box to put them in tonight.")

Sammy Goldstein threw up in class and we all had to wait outside in the hall until the janitor came. Sammy was a Jew.

Life magazine did a picture article on birth, but we weren't allowed to see it.

And still every year Harry brought us pennies, hundreds of pennies, in two old socks.

"Tough."

"What's tough?"

"Life."

"What's Life?"

"Magazine."

"How Much?"

"Ten Cents."

"I've only got a nickel."

"Tough."

"What's tough?"

"Life."

The day that President Roosevelt died I was upstairs making a mummy for our Social Studies project, had an old doll, a roll of adhesive tape, some flower petals, cotton wool and a shoebox. I had just covered up the box when Leslie, whose brother was a paper boy and had been called in to deliver the Extra, came running up the street to tell us. It seemed very significant to me that I should be working on death when the President had just passed away. I finished covering up the rest of the face and placed the mummy gently in its sarcophagus. It must have been springtime, for I remember I was using quince apple blossoms to cover the body with. Leslie invited Jane and me for supper. They were having pancakes. Yet I don't remember a word that either of my parents said. He was a Democrat, like my father, but an aristocrat and so very suspect. Did they mourn him, I wonder, or did they feel he'd "sold us down the river at Yalta" — a phrase I was to hear a lot, much later?

I wrote a poem about the unknown solder and read it out, voice shaking, at assembly:

> As solemn faces pass my
> tomb
> I lie within my world of
> gloom.

(It was very well received.)

We listened to the Lucky Strike Hit Parade and sent away for pamphlets on "Florida, your postwar vacation dreamland."

(Mae-Love leaned against the butcher's counter with her lard-white arms. Harry sat with us at Camp of the Woods on Sunday morning, a curious smile on his lips, as she ran lightly down the stone steps to be counted among the saved.

"STAND UP, STAND UP FOR JESUS, YE SOLDIERS OF THE CROSS."

"Sister Woolcock," the reverend cried, embracing her, "it's just wonderful to see you here this morning!")

But when the war in the Pacific ended we knew nothing about it until Harry sent me running up the road to knock at the front door of the Daley's camp. We had not seen a paper in a week or listened to the radio because it had gone on the blink. Therefore we did not know about the "Enola Gay" or the 90,000 killed in Hiroshima, the 40,000 killed at Nagasaki, the mushroom cloud, the screams, the blown figures melting in the heat. First we saw only fireworks and celebration.

4:35

I came back and told them that the war was over, triumphant, running down the sandy road barefoot (and yet at the same time observing Isobel, messenger of glad tidings, running down the road in faded shorts and summer-toughened feet).

Harry said "Go and unlock the gun closet" and gave me the

key. He took out a bottle he called "the Pope's telephone number" and poured everybody a drink, even Jane and me. It was the first time I had ever seen him take a drink or even seen my parents touch anything but Christmas wine, but it was so exciting because the war was over and at last the boys could come home. I ran out to the big bell on the porch and rang it over and over again so everyone would know we were happy too even though we didn't have any fireworks. Then Harry locked the whiskey up again and said it was no use being a damn fool about this, but he gave the hired man the rest of the day off so he could go and celebrate with his folks.

My father took the old bugle off the wall and played Taps with tears in his eyes for all the boys who wouldn't be coming back, and our dog Skipper howled and howled until Mother took her and shut her up in the workshop, where her howls still came up, sepulchral, from below. Daddy played it again, and better this time, and the sound floated over the lake and up into the sun-bright afternoon. Harry had a pure silk Jap parachute that someone had given him and I asked what would happen to the Japanese. He said, "Well, I don't think they'll want to believe in the Rising Sun again."

Nobody quarrelled that night. It was very still.

When the UN was formed and we celebrated the first UN Day at school, our principal, a bitter man with a club foot, went from class to class to get some ethnic diversity for the coming school assembly.

"Why not Isobel Cleary for Ireland?" suggested the teacher. My heart thudded in hope. In dread.

"Shanty Irish," he said, and the teacher laughed because it was the principal making a joke. "Shanty Irish."

If I had had a German bayonet I would have run him through.

"Hold still, dear," said the dentist, turning on the drill. "Just raise your hand if I'm hurting you and we'll take a breather."

Later, as I spat blood and silver into the swirling water: "Would you tell your mother we'd like a little something on account?" I could hear the noise of the street beyond the venetian blinds.

"Did you know your aquarium's filthy?" I asked the nurse. "Disgusting." And walked out.

nine

My parents never had any casual visitors. There was Harry, of course, every Christmas and on alternative Thanksgivings, Aunt Olive when she happened to come to town. Maybe the minister once or twice, but I don't remember it. Aunt Hepzie and Aunt Charlotte, the downstate aunts, who lived now on Staten Island, came once a year to visit Uncle Pudge's family in Oneonta as well as Aunt Olive in Syracuse and ourselves. They were both large women, spinsters, my grandfather Cleary's elder sisters. They wore black crêpe dresses and black laced shoes, smelled of cough drops and eau de cologne. They never actually stayed with us but rather chose the Belmont Hotel, right next to the railway station, where they would be assured of biscuits and morning tea and a doctor if one of them should have a sudden attack in the night. I remember only that Charlotte was the fatter of the two and more timid (therefore more approachable) and that Aunt Hepzie always wore a mourning ring made out of human hair. They gave us marvellous dresses: a sailor dress with a real whistle, a party dress with a hand-smocked yoke, polka dot dresses with matching coats, pink for Jane, blue for me. How they could know about such things was beyond me. But they also gave us lectures on deportment — it was obvious that Mother wasn't bringing us up quite right.

We sat on the edges of our chairs, very straight, earning our new dresses.

"Never slouch, dear, it's bad for the digestion."

Also came Arnold Savery, an old school chum of my father's who checked on our house, sometimes, during the summer when we were away and mended the furnace. Things like that. He wore a red plaid shirt, work trousers and a peaked cap — like a hunter. My mother hated him.

"What's Arnold Savery doing in that get-up?"

"What get-up?"

"The hunting outfit. I should think the only thing he's ever hunted for is his mama's bifocals."

Arnold scraped his work boots extra hard on the door mat and went straight down with my father to see what was wrong with the thermostat.

"Nothing he fixes ever lasts long anyway. I don't know why we can't have a proper electrician in."

Arnold seemed to us both feeble-minded ("Ay-uh," he always said, like some backwoodsman, "ay-uh, we'll have a look at it") and uninteresting.

Then there were the bill collectors: the Dairyland man, the insurance man, God knows who else. But they stood in the hall and talked to my father (if he was home). Otherwise we hid until they went away. I can still recognize the back of a bill collector's shoulders.

When I was about twelve I gave my parents, for Christmas, a little wooden box with a door on it and a pad and pencil inside. They hung it up just outside the front door, above the bell. It said, "If at home you do not find us, leave a note that will remind us." But no one ever used it — ever.

My father went to the Masons or to school, but he never brought his friends or colleagues home. Our mother went no place, and not even the neighbours were invited over for a cup of coffee. In the eighteen-odd years I lived "at home" (if only on the holidays), they *never*, together or separately, had a real guest in for the evening. I couldn't believe the dinner parties that some of my schoolmates talked about. Instead, my father worked on his garden or went up to his room and marked or practised for one of his Degrees. My mother lay across her bed and read her books and magazines. And nobody ever just dropped in to see us. That's why the incident with the smelts remains so vividly in my memory.

Leslie Macdonald was my sister's age and lived just down the street from us in a big, old rambling house with a verandah on which we used to play on rainy days. Leslie's mother had been a Whitehead, which was a very good thing to be, for Grandfather Whitehead had held a lot of stock in MacLeod's and Leslie could still take things to the counter and show a little card and say "shareholder's discount please." But Daisy Whitehead had married beneath her, a handsome, no-good man who turned out to be an alcoholic. Everybody knew about Leslie's father, who went away periodically for "cures." Mrs. Macdonald drank too and her face had begun to melt. She couldn't always remember where the prizes had been put at birthday parties. Leslie called her mother's boyfriends Uncle this and Uncle that and I was always rather afraid of her mother because of the faint smell of liquor on her breath (neither of my parents drank except for a little Virginia Dare or Manischewitz in the fruit cocktail at Christmas time) and her rather eccentric behaviour. One day she sat us down and insisted we eat a plateful of saltines and leftover cocktail sauce. And once she tried to teach me to do the Charleston. But we felt a kinship with Leslie, not just because she lived on the same street but because we felt that she, too, was a casualty in the game of life. She had a brother — much older — named Alasdair — but we rarely saw him and so she seemed just as alone as we were.

Throughout our grammar school years the three of us played together: Stone School, Fish, Old Maid, Jacks, Hide and Seek. ("One Potato/ Two Potato/ Three Potato/Four/ Five Potato/Six

Potato/ Seven Potato or.") We exchanged dirty book titles —
The Yellow River by I.P. Daly. Hole in the Mattress by I. Mister
Compleatly — and daydreams. Leslie was going to be an airline
stewardess, Jane a veterinarian, I a poet. She had a marvellous
doll's house on the second-storey landing, and her mother never
minded if we took dabs of perfume from the cutglass bottles on
her dressing table or borrowed her dancing shoes. *Our* mother
said Daisy simply "made do" on what the Whiteheads had left
her, and "Your father may not be much but at least he's not a
drinking man like Archie Macdonald."

Mother had gone to Central High with Archie. He was vale-
dictorian the year she was salutatorian (whatever that meant)
and came on stage in a witch's costume to tell the futures of the
individual members of the class. I doubt if she had said more
than "hello" or "goodbye" to him since then, so it was very
strange when we came back from the store one day and saw him
stumbling up our front steps with a bucket in his hand.

"Slow down," Jane said. "That's Leslie's dad going up our
front steps."

"I know."

"He's drunk."

"So what's new?"

"Mother will never let him in."

But she did. And a few minutes later we came in quietly
behind him. They were in the kitchen and Mother was laughing
in a forced, half-frightened way. We stood in the dining room
and watched dumbfounded. Mr. Macdonald was hanging onto
the gas range as though it might disappear at any moment.
Mother was very red-faced, her arms covered in flour, a half-
finished apple pie in front of her.

"Listen to me, Clara. Nobody listens to me. I've brought you
some smelts. Fresh-caught. Perfect for your supper." He leaned
over and grabbed a handful from the bucket, letting them drop
back through his open fingers.

It was the most exciting thing that had happened in our
house since Mother tore up Aunt Olive's twenty dollar bill. We
were fascinated. Here was our friend's father, our mother's old

schoolmate, drunk and hardly able to stand upright, invading our mother's kitchen.

What would she do? What say? Smelts. Even the word sounded vaguely obscene, and he kept repeating it. "Here y'are, Clara. Some nice fresh smelts. Got 'em m'self at Chenango Lake." The fish dropped back in the bucket with little smacking sounds, like kisses.

My mother came forward and pushed at Mr. Macdonald with her floury hands, leaving chalk marks on his jacket. Her face was as red as though she had been sitting in front of a fire.

"Get out, Archie. Do you want me to call the paddy wagon?" But laughing. We were confused.

"You don' understand. I've brought you some smelts. Aren't they lovely?" Tears rolled down his face.

"Get out. You're a fool. You ought to be ashamed. Have you no consideration for your wife and children?"

"Sure," he said. "Sure." And staggered past us, unseeing, leaving his bucket behind. After he had gone my mother wrapped up the little fish in yesterday's paper and took them out to the garbage can.

My father, when he came home, was really interested.

"Smelts, hey? I haven't had those in years. What'd you throw them out for? We could've rolled 'em in corn meal and fried 'em."

"I don't want any presents from a half-dead alcoholic, thank you very much." We were sitting around waiting for the pie to finish cooking. "If you want them get them yourself."

Mr. Macdonald never bothered us again. Once I saw him fall out of a taxi just as it rolled up in front of his house. We were playing skip with Leslie and pretended not to notice as the taxi driver got out and came around to help his passenger up the stairs. Shortly after that he went away and never came back again. Mrs. Macdonald filed for a divorce, and from my mother's attitude I found it very difficult to tell which was worse — an alcoholic or a divorcee. Leslie, Alasdair and their mother moved to a smaller house on Beethoven Street, but Jane and Leslie remained friends for a long, long time.

And then, one summer, years later, we went to get the mail. There were several letters for Harry, one for Daddy (readdressed and probably a bill), *Life* magazine and a pink envelope for Jane, from Leslie. Jane wanted to sit down and read it right then, but I was getting hot, so took the wild flowers we'd gathered and the rest of the mail and walked on ahead. Suddenly Jane called to me.

"Isobel. Come here. Leslie's father's dead." She stood there, her face white under its tan, in the middle of the sleepy summer afternoon.

I ran back. "What happened? Did he have an accident?"

"No. He was in a sanitarium and he killed himself. With a razor."

We looked at each other and saw nothing: no reassurance, no comfort, only incredulity. There, on the sandy path, with butterflies fluttering around us and a blue sky overhead, we were supposed to believe in somebody called "Leslie's father" who had killed himself with a razor! I turned up my own wrists, still pale, the blue veins showing just beneath the surface. To want to, yes. but actually to dare? To let your blood run out like wine?

I remember him drunk, the smelts falling through his fingers, a handsome man. Haunted by what?

The only visitor we ever had; and I think he came up our front steps by mistake.

ten

9:01
9:02
9:03

'48, '49, '50
("Isobel, where have you been?"
"At the park."
"What were you doing?"
"Nothing. Riding the merry-go-round."
"Were you alone?"
"Of course."
Pictures of Clara weeping as the ΦΚ pledges went by in their brown and orange beanies, singing.

"I don't understand it, I don't understand it. I've always done my best. Why, I knew Mary Lou Whelan's mother when she was nothing. Nothing! There's no need for her to put on airs."

My father, nervous and sad behind his evening paper — "It's a goddamned shame."

"Mother, I do not *choose* to be alone!"

What did we do all those years? Ashamed of one another, hating one another, blaming one another. Outcasts, misfits, our misery spread like the damp along the walls.

"Think I'll just walk the dog around the block."

"Warne....Warne!"

"Wha?"

"Bring us back some doughnuts and a bottle of ginger-ale."

Crying into my pillow, "My punishment is more than I can bear!")

But still, we spent our summers in the mountains.

eleven

My first real love was a boy named Christopher Meyer from Johnstown, New York, and I met him, naturally, in the mountains. At the first summer dance I ever went to. Always before my sister and I had lain in the darkness in the old double bed, listening to the distant music coming from the Fish and Game Club every Saturday night. It came in our open window all summer long, faint and far away like dream music: scratchy violins and the thud-thud-thud of a bass, competing against the crickets, the bull frogs in the creek, the snores of our mother and father. Music enticing but nothing to do with us. Sometimes, if the wind was right, a sudden burst of unexplained laughter, as though two worlds had overlapped for a brief second in time. We lay under our flannelette sheets, curled into each other like two thin, brown question marks, her front in my back, her arms around my waist, our long sun-bleached hair spread out like honey or starfish on the pillowcases the housekeeper had trimmed with tatting so many years ago.

Lay thus for many summers and were content with the awareness of our own strength and health, the immortality of tomorrow's sunrise, the masked raccoons out there in the fragrant darkness, working away skilfully at the garbage can lids my grandfather and the hired man had wired on for the twenty-ninth time that summer. Of these sounds the music was perhaps the most minor, the most expendable.

But the summer I fell in love was different from all that, right from the very beginning. First, my father decided to take a summer job travelling for a seed company in the Southern states. It was so out of character for him that I was stunned. He hated driving, drove slowly and cautiously, one foot hovering over the brake, sweating his way up hills, cursing his way along highways. Add to this that he loved the cottage and going out fishing early in the morning, bringing back trout or perch for breakfast, cooking them himself on the old potbelly stove. Milk and egg first, then cornmeal. Fried in hot bacon fat. I felt my mother had shamed him into it, as we were constantly in debt and because he was a teacher she felt he should "get off his backside" and earn some money in the summers. We may have been more in debt than usual that summer, or perhaps I misread the situation now, looking back down "the wrong end of the telescope of time." Perhaps he had decided to have an adventure come what may, to get away from my mother and her endless complaints about his inadequacies, even from us whom he loved in his own inarticulate, hesitant way, away from the contempt we had been brought up to feel for him. Certainly, he liked meeting people — we would sit in the car outside a service station or roadside stand, fuming, while he "gassed" (as my mother put it) and "made a fool of himself." "Warren," she would call, "Warne," and start honking the horn, which embarrassed us just as much as our father's prolixity. The horn would honk, the dog would bark and our father, deep into local weather conditions or the merits of Golden Bantam over all other varieties of corn or questions on how the fish were bitin', would glance around, startled, blinking his eyes. "Guess the missus wants to get goin'." Also, he liked growing things. Seeds were probably more attractive than encyclopedias or Fuller brushes. And he liked to feel important — God knows he didn't get any help from home in that direction — would have an expense account and be able to stay in hotels and to sign himself "W.G. Cleary, Sales Representative" in the hotel register.

At any rate he was due to set out the first week in July, was already worrying about the traffic on the Fourth and whether our old Buick would take the hills. Bought himself a seersucker jacket (on credit) and a new straw hat. My mother decided to spend the first month in town (again, not quite in character) and leave us in the hands of our grandfather and Aunt Hettie, who had returned at last to the home of her father and was keeping house for him in town. She was a large, fat woman who wore a lavalier and embarrassed us terribly by getting her name on the religious page of the local paper.

Sister Harriet Goodenough
Tonight at the City Mission
"Except ye Become as Little Children"
8 P.M.
All Welcome

Sometimes her picture as well. She brought drunks home and fed them in the kitchen, singing all the while. Took weird old ladies with names like Violet Rubber or Mary-Beth Darling out for rides in Harry's car.

Brought us up jars of chicken stock or home-made grape juice. Walked right in without knocking and told us how she'd been "saved" one night in Darien. We hated and feared her without quarter.

So here were all those changes before we even got to the cottage. Driving up through the sleepy little villages, past all the farms and familiar landmarks ("Look, they've changed the Burma Shave sign"), old posters, like peeling skin, against the weathered barns. No stopping at Jose's stand in Utica for hamburgers and milkshakes. Aunt Hettie had prepared chopped egg sandwiches and lemonade. We ate by the side of the road, quickly, with the car doors open, our old spaniel tied to the door handle with a bit of clothesline. Folded the grease-proof paper so it could be used again and listened to grace, even over lousy chopped egg sandwiches. (My sister poked her elbow in my ribs.)

And arriving in daylight, too, which I couldn't remember ever having done before. My grandfather very silent and concentrated as he drove, but competent, not uneasy, Aunt Hettie singing hymns in a nasal, off-key voice. Always before our grandfather and the housekeeper went up a week or so ahead of time and his reassuring figure was now at the top of the back steps, mythical against the light, the smell of dew-softened pine needles and the promise of the lake below. Fresh coffee ground by hand and put to perk when they heard our car down the road. This time it was afternoon and all the big padlocks were in place. Aunt Hettie, in flowered dress and sensible shoes, her glasses bumping against her bosom, eased her great bulk out of the car and began giving orders at once. Only the dog was allowed to run free and renew her sensuous acquaintance with the forest. We carried in boxes of groceries, the ice chest, bed linen and the crime magazines my grandfather read every evening, seated by the big old-fashioned wireless whose dial gave false promises of news from Tokyo, Hong Kong, Madrid or London. (The most we ever got was Utica or Hamilton, New York.) The cabin smelled of damp. There were cobwebs, and last year's flypaper, with a few of last year's flies dried onto it like dried-up currants or raisins, hung forlornly from the ceiling. A field mouse had unravelled one of my old pullovers and laid her babies in a dresser drawer. They set up a tiny but terrible squeaking when I opened it. I took them out carefully, wool and all, and put them behind the woodpile, hoping their mother would find them and the cocker spaniel wouldn't. Down below the sunlight flashed us signals off the water and we swept and scrubbed rebelliously until Aunt Hettie was satisfied and had sat down on the porch swing to rest and read her Bible. In the little bathroom, between my grandfather's room and the room now used for housekeepers, she had placed her dental floss, her iron tablets, her flowered "sponge bag" as she called it, her tube of

Squibb toothpaste. Her extra pair of sensible black shoes stuck out from underneath the chintz bedspread like the feet of the Wicked Witch of the West. She had taken down the Varga girls, who had been tacked up on the wall for as long as I could remember, and replaced them with a picture of Jesus blessing the children. I was uneasy and rather depressed, the way I had felt when Christmas Day rolled around the first year I had discovered there was no Santa Claus. I was afraid Aunt Hettie's presence might colour my reaction to what had been, up to now, an almost transcendental relationship to the cabin and its surroundings. Grandpa had lit a big fire to take the chill off, but still I felt cold and vaguely unhappy. Things were changing, had changed already, and I felt shoved along against my will. I helped my sister run up the flag on the flagpole and then we made our escape to the beach. Down there it was better. We unlocked the boathouse and were reassured to find all the old familiar things just as we had left them: the three boats, the fishing rods, the dart board, the badminton set and beach umbrella, the faded kapok-stuffed cushions we used as life preservers, a set of bows and arrows (never used), a selection of oars in brackets against one wall. Red cans with gooseneck spouts for kerosene and gas, the big tin medicine kit which contained, among other things, a little snakebite set complete with razor blade and suction tube and gauze-covered glass vial of something you broke if anyone had a heart attack. We sat on the front step and shared a package of Necco wafers. It was the very end of the heat of the day and the sweat trickled down the backs of our bare legs.

The lake was beside us, the creek behind the boathouse, the warm, biscuit-coloured sand beneath our feet. To the west, on the other side of the lake, we could see Panther Mountain crouched eternally beneath the sky. All was utterly still. Even the faint, rusty "creak-creak" of the porch glider had stopped: Aunt Hettie had fallen asleep. We cheered up. The summer waited for us, still furled like the faded flag above us on the rise.

"Let's take a boat out."

"Let's."

"D'you think we should tell Aunt Hettie?"

"She's asleep. Safe in the arms of Jesus."

"I'll row," I said. (I'd heard it would increase my bust.)

The days established themselves in a certain pattern. Early in the morning, as in previous summers, our grandfather would get up and light a fire in the big fireplace and start the potbelly stove. We would lie in our flannelette nest, the room taking shape like a vision around us, our breath steaming in the cold when we stuck our heads out of the covers. Grandpa's footsteps went down the back steps to check on his kingdom. Replaced by Aunt Hettie's heavier tread as she came through from the other side of the house, singing. ("I've got that extra-special Sunday feeling deep in my heart, deep in my heart, deep in my heart.") As she didn't really like the cabin or the woods this always seemed blatant hypocrisy. Thud. The big yellow bowl, for mixing the pancakes, was on the counter. Slam. The icebox on the back porch opened and shut. Milk. Eggs. We fished out our blue jeans and shirts, which we kept under the covers at the foot of the bed, and ran as fast as we could to the front room and the fire. It was ridiculous — no, impossible — to believe that the temperature would be in the 80s by afternoon. Our cold hands were an affront to our bodies as we fumbled out of our nightgowns and into our clothes.

Aunt Hettie's bifocals winked at us from the kitchen. "Did you girls wash?"

"No, Aunt Hettie."

"Well, you go and wash right now — a good wash — not one of your slapdash affairs." ("Deep in my heart, deep in my heart." She had on an old grey man's cardigan over her flowered dress. Mixing the pancake batter with a wooden spoon.)

We squeezed fresh oranges in a peculiar grey metal squeezer, rather like an earth mover's shovel, that I've never seen the like of since. Real oranges. Maybe a dozen for the four of us. Emptied maple syrup from the five-gallon tin into a glass syrup jug. Set out butter and ground the coffee beans. Aunt Hettie would ask us about our dreams and whether we'd had a BM. She had written a letter to one of her friends doing the Lord's work in Northern Rhodesia and would we run up and mail it in time to catch the truck. She told us stories of her days at Bible college or when she worked with the lost souls in Hackensack Women's Reformatory. The pile of pancakes, warm under two tea towels, grew higher as she talked. Her voice, when she spoke to us, was almost too sweet, like the maple syrup; and the point of most of her stories was how she, by giving herself to Jesus, had been able to triumph over anyone and anything.

We ate, Grandpa at the head of the long table. Enormous quantities of pancakes, sometimes with leftover corn or blueberries in them. Rivers of maple syrup. Stoking up for the day. Then did the dishes quickly, arguing over who would wash and who would dry, made the beds and swept. Aunt Hettie was turning out all the cupboards, getting together a box of "odds and ends" to send to a mission in Asia.

"Aunt Hettie, that pullover belongs to Mother."

"This old thing! She'll never miss it!" And old swimming suits from our pygmy past. Two little pinafores trimmed in eyelet lace that she found in a cabin trunk. A perfectly good pair of shoes that the last housekeeper had left behind. But careful not to go into my grandfather's room or presume too much. Always singing or humming as she worked, a motley collection of songs and hymns from all the various persuasions she'd tested and found wanting. But favoured the evangelical stuff. "I like a hymn with a bit of body to it." Down on her knees with her head in a cupboard, her vast flowered behind an almost unbearable temptation.

We spent most of our time on the lake, coming in only when Grandpa or Aunt Hettie rang the old brass bell which hung from a beam on the front porch. I would row as hard as I could, out, out and away, until the boathouse (painted with aluminum paint) was shining shape rather than definite structure, the cottage something understood behind a pine-tree-covered hill. We trailed our hands in the water and drifted. My sister would pull off her tee shirt and dungarees and turn her face up to the sun. She wore what was then a very daring two piece and I envied her those swelling breasts, blue-white like skim milk or finest marble. My own bathing suit, the colour of a setting sun, seemed less glamorous than when I had tried it on in the shop. I closed my eyes and tried not to care. Hello, Sky. Hello, Lake. I cupped my hand and then let the cool water run through like liquid pleasure. It was very strange to think of my father, some nervous speck on an unknown Southern highway, my mother a hundred and fifty miles away in town. Doing what? I couldn't really imagine what one would do, in the city, in the summer. The boat circled slowly. Like a feather. Like our lives.

On Friday my sister said suddenly, from beneath her sailor hat, "I want to go to the dance tomorrow night."

"What d'you mean?"

"The square dance, stupid. At the Fish and Game Club. I want to go."

I sat up and tied my straps. "Aunt Hettie would never let us."

"Grandpa would."

"I'm not so sure." (Harry, although a great practical joker and lenient in some ways, neither smoked nor drank and kept strict hours.)

"You wait and see."

From far away came the insistent clang of the dinner bell.

"I'll bet you fifty cents he won't."

"I'll bet you fifty cents he will."

But he did not. She began the following day at lunch, waiting until grace had been said and Aunt Hettie was passing the fried chicken.

"I was wondering, Grandpa, if Isobel and I could go to the square dance tonight."

Aunt Hettie put down the platter with a thump, but my grandfather continued to cut up his salad (half a head of lettuce, vinegar and oil in crystal cruets, a dusting of salt and sugar every day of every summer as far back as I could remember) without speaking.

"Why, would you want to do that, honey? Haven't you young'uns got enough to do around here? Some folks don't know when they're well off." Rolling her eyes heavenward and joking with the Lord. Her flypaper voice did not deceive. Nor did her flypaper smile.

114

I kicked my sister under the table, but she went on, calmly.

"We would enjoy going. We have never been."

"I should think not!" Rolling her eyes at the Lord again. "Your mama has some crazy notions but she's not that crazy."

I was cold again and picked at the edge of the table where the oilcloth had worn thin. My grandfather continued to cut up his lettuce with a surgeon's precision. Then he looked up, sharply, his eyes two blue flames. But could turn cold, like polar ice.

"How do you propose to get there?" (My sister pressed her leg against mine, triumphantly.)

"We walk farther than that when we walk into Trinity."

He nodded his head and placed the salad to the right of his dinner plate. Helped himself to chicken and boiled potatoes but no milk gravy.

"But not at night."

"And not to a dance hall," cried Aunt Hettie, forgetting, in her zeal, that you don't talk with your mouth full. Beating her plate with a drumstick. "Cer-tain-ly-not-to-a-dance-hall."

"It's not really a dance hall, Aunt Hettie. People just dance there once a week. Square dances. On Saturday nights."

"Dance with the devil when you're sixteen," she cried, "where will you be when you're twenty?"

Behind my grandfather's chair, nailed to the wall, was a salmon he had caught on his first trip to the Canadian Rockies. On the plaque was a little metal sign that read, "I wouldn't be here if I had kept my mouth shut."

"Never mind *that*," said my grandfather. "The point is, I don't want to cart you there and go and get you. It's too late."

"But we said we'd *walk*," my sister protested.

"And I say you won't. Pass me down the corn if you please."

"Here you are, Dad." Aunt Hettie gave us a look of self-righteous spite, began to hum under her breath.

So that on Saturday we lay as we always did, in the big old double bed, faded pictures of kittens with balls of wool, puppies in baskets, marching unseen around the walls. As we always had before. But different this time, the music closer, more insistent, more enticing.

"The old bitch."

"Fucking old maid." (Shocking both of us.)

"But it's Grandpa, too. He could take us if he wanted to." (They were playing "San Antonio Rose." Aunt Hettie had asked if we wanted to go along to the Camp of the Woods revival meeting in Excelsior in the morning.)

"I'm damn well not going to stay here cooped up like some prisoner the whole damned summer. I'd rather be back in town."

I disagreed but was terribly depressed. Already the summer was chipped and cracked like something precious that couldn't bear rough handling. We lay apart, our backs to one another.

The next week my sister spent most of her time spread-eagled on an old blanket, slathering herself with Johnson's baby oil. She said she was "bored" with going out on the lake and began writing daily letters to her best friend back in town. So I went out by myself, rowing farther and farther away. Or took the boat with the motor, going as far as the little island on the east side of the lake, circling it, looking down at the sharp rocks just below the surface. (One summer a motorboat had tipped over there and a young man from Batavia had had both his legs torn off by the propeller. My sister had told me the legs were still down there, caught under a ledge of rock, and I had believed her. She had also told me marmalade was made from goldfish.)

Aunt Hettie, in her white perforated summer shoes, cooked and cleaned or read the Bible sitting on the screened-in porch, her fat legs up on a pillow, stockingless (her one concession to the summer). She was a fanatical housekeeper and even kept my grandfather's starched shirts and detachable collars rolled up in the icebox before she ironed them. We had to rinse our feet whenever we went in the house. I hated the sound and feel of the sand against the sides of the enamel pan she kept just inside the back porch door. If we said we were hungry, she said, "Can you eat a cold potato? You're not really hungry, young'un, unless you can eat a cold potato." We missed the succession of bizarre but kindly housekeepers my grandfather had employed before the Lord told Aunt Hettie her place was with her father. For the first time my grandfather, who had seemed as unchanging, as eternal as the summer sun, began to look really old. He had death spots on the back of his hands — were they there last year? the year before? — and he sometimes fell asleep in his chair. Aunt Hettie packed away his juice glasses with the girls who had disappearing costumes on them. She took down the cartoon he had found, years ago, in *Esquire*. A fat lady leaving an executive's office: "For the last time, Mr. Goodenough, my name is Marie, not Fanny." Sat on the edge of our bed at night and prayed for us, asked if we had ever before known what it was like to live in a Christian home. Declared we didn't need a washwoman; the girls and I can do it all quite easily once a week.

Then one afternoon in the second week I came back from a trip around the island to find my sister (who had been particularly gloomy that day and was threatening to join her girlfriend in the Poconos) sitting up on the old Indian blanket which served as a beach towel, a smug expression on her face.

"D'you still want to go to the square dances?"

"I dunno. I guess so." (What I really wanted was for things to go back to where they were a year ago.)

"Well, wait until suppertime and see what happens."

"What have you been up to?"

"Wait and see."

We went up the path to the cottage, feet already toughened to the burning sand but the path through the woods cool and soothing just the same. My sister offered to help Aunt Hettie shell the peas — "Now that's real Christian of you, honey." I thought they were both pretty sickening and went away to the old outhouse, no longer used except to store old Sears, Roebuck catalogues or newspapers — useful for starting fires. I sat on the covered-over seat and sulked. On the wall was another one of my grandfather's practical jokes — a red metal box with a corn cob in it and a sign: "In case of emergency, break glass." It seemed strange that Aunt Hettie was his daughter. My mother had told me Aunt Hettie drank iodine, once, in New York. That was incredible too. We were supposed to feel sorry for her — at least that's what I gathered. Old maids married Jesus.

Grandfather had "warped" her (that was my mother's word). It was all so difficult. My mother didn't like my father, but was it better to be married than to be an old maid?? In the card game you lost if you got the Old Maid. What *I* really wanted to do was to remain forever fixed, with the cottage, the lake, the sky in a summer afternoon of my own choosing — like the little girl in the glass paperweight at home. But life wouldn't leave me alone. ("In case of Emergency, break glass.") An indifferent spider continued building her web above my head.

At supper my sister offered to say grace. "For what we are about to receive, may the Lord make us truly thankful." (And kicked me under the table.) "Amen," said Aunt Hettie, loudly, in case God might not hear her. I was getting very suspicious. Over dessert, which was Blueberry Grunt (my grandpa's favourite, and fixed by my sister, I suspected, particularly for tonight), she dropped her bombshell.

"Grandpa," she said, "I went for a walk up the beach today and met the Daleys' son and daughter-in-law."

"Is that so?" His mind was on the dessert and on the roof, which had to be repaired in the morning.

"Yes. They offered to take Isobel and me to the square dance Saturday night."

My grandfather said nothing, but his blue eyes flared.

"And?"

"And I said I'd ask your permission. They aren't going to stay very late."

I watched Aunt Hettie, not my grandfather. The blueberries had stained her lips purple, and because her face had gone very red, she looked like she might be having a heart attack. Gave the funny clearing of her throat and cough, which passed with her, for laughter.

"I thought we settled all that, honey." My sister returned her purple smile.

"Not really. Grandpa only said he couldn't take us because it was too late."

"Now look here, Dad...." She moved her smile to the right. The hired man, who had been invited to supper, ate head down and earnestly, not wanting to be involved. Aunt Hettie hoped to save him before the summer's end.

My grandfather wiped his mouth with his napkin and pushed back his chair.

"You have to be back by eleven sharp and lock up when you come in."

Aunt Hettie licked her purple lips, speechless. The hired man squeezed silently behind her, gave a little nod and hurriedly disappeared.

"You're going to let them go?"

"Why not?"

"You know very well why not!"

"I don't want to hear another word about it. Girls, do the washing up."

He went out on the porch to sit and wait for the sunset. Aunt Hettie remained at the table, her lips moving silently. We began to clear the table, not arguing as usual. I knew we had won for the wrong reasons, that my grandfather was letting us go to spite Aunt Hettie. This bothered me even though I was more or less used to being a pawn in my parents' quarrels. When we went out to take down the flag she was still there, praying, head bowed now, mumbling at her lap. A red sun, enormously swollen, burst and stained the evening sky. My sister shrugged and pulled me into our bedroom to talk about what we'd wear. Then we lay together on our stomachs, in companionable silence, reading a copy of *True Detective*, a thing our mother (as well as Aunt Hettie) really frowned on. There were always headless bodies in sacks, or corpses being raised from abandoned wells. The moon came up and peered over our shoulder and I was glad that Grandpa hadn't agreed to let us walk to the dance. The dark outside seemed suddenly full of sinister implications. We stared at photographs of country sheriffs and loungers present at the scenes of discovery, axes and shotguns, a hand holding up a pickle jar that had contained rat poison. And should have had bad dreams, but didn't. Our aunt, for the first time, failed to come in and say good night.

On Saturday night, in peasant blouses and beautifully

starched gingham skirts, we set off for the dance with young Mr. and Mrs. Daley. They came in and said hello to my grandfather (it was the first time I could remember any of the neighbours ever having come onto our property) and to Aunt Hettie, who gave them one of her pitying smiles and rocked slowly back and forth in our dead grandma's rocking chair.

"On about the devil's business, young'uns. On about the devil's business!" Embarrassed but determined, we put on our shoes, picked up our cardigans and made a hasty exit.

"Please don't mind our aunt," said my sister from the back seat of the car and speaking in a phoney, grown-up voice. "She had a nervous breakdown when she was young and has never been quite right since." I was surprised at this betrayal of our aunt — it was one thing for us to despise her, quite another to drag these two strangers into it. But the young couple — "Beatty and Jim," said my sister, introducing us — just made an appropriate murmur and didn't pursue the subject. I got the feeling they might not have been going to the dance if my sister hadn't somehow talked them into it.

How strange it seemed to be driving *away* from the cottage at night, down the narrow sand-packed side road, past all my grandfather's joking signs — "No U Turn," "Men Working," "Hospital. Slow," picked out by the glare of the headlights. We went past the row of mailboxes at the end (ours a replica of the boathouse), all the red flags down, and turned right toward Excelsior. Through the open windows and over the sound of a million crickets the music drew us on. "Come. Come. Come. Come." The thud of the bass fiddle was a combination of the frogs and my beating heart.

And we were there, very nervous now as we went up the rickety porch steps with Beatty in her dirndl skirt and Jim in his short-sleeve summer shirt. Past men in work boots and lumber jackets, a woman with a shrill laugh, her cardigan out at the elbows. Inside all was noise and bright lights and whirling figures. ("Meet that pretty girl, pass her by. Hook the next girl on the fly.") I wanted to hold my sister's hand but knew she would slap me or, worse still, walk away. She seemed to have acquired a new boldness in the past two weeks. The Daleys pushed a way through the loungers around the makeshift bar and hot dog stand and led us to a bench along one wall where we sat and waited for a new set to begin. There were a lot of middle-aged couples, men with paunches in grey or slate-blue work shirts, string ties with fancy clasps. Women in flowered skirts, white socks and black court pumps. A square made up of college kids who summered at the other end of our lake — boys in white duck trousers and white sports shirts, very tanned, girls with long brown, graceful legs and fraternity or sorority pins on their peasant blouses. The fire warden's two fat daughters were dancing with each other, and over in the far corner — we nudged each other — was Willie B., our grandfather's hired man, with one of the local girls. ("The gents swing out, the ladies swing in. Form that Texas star ag'in.") Children chased each other in and out of the washrooms, and there was a rather unpleasant smell of beer and sweat and the hot dogs which sold for a nickel apiece, benefit of the VFD. It didn't seem very promising and I began to feel our victory over Aunt Hettie was, if not Pyrrhic, a dubious one at best.

The music stopped; the fiddlers wiped their gleaming foreheads, the pianist took a swig from a bottle on top of the upright piano and the bass player picked out a few deep notes, absentmindedly — as one might pick at his nose — while he talked to some of his pals. When the next set started ("Choose your partners, ladies and gemmen, choose your partners") Beatty and Jim, with apologetic smiles, left us, to make the fourth couple in a square on the other side of the room. The caller tapped his heel and cleared his throat. The fiddlers put a last lick of resin on their bows and tucked their fiddles snugly under their chins. We were left sitting against the wall. ("Honour your partners. Honour your corners. All join hands and circle left.")

"D'you want a hot dog?" I asked miserably.

"Are you kidding?"

"This was your bright idea. You needn't be so snotty."

"Shut up."

"You shut up."

All said between clenched teeth, identical smiles on our faces. ("Dosey-doh with your corner, dosey-doh with your partner, grab your partner for the grand promenade.")

I was all for walking home. Beatty and Jim, who had seemed so drab and married, were laughing and swinging away to beat the band while my sister and I sat on the sidelines with the old women and sleeping babies. I knew Jim would ask us each to dance in turn — he seemed that sort of person — but it wouldn't be the same. And then, halfway through "Red River Valley" (my favourite), a group of teenage boys came lumbering in, all arms and legs and averted eyes. A man of about the same age as the Daleys was with them and a very pretty young woman I'd seen before at the general store in Excelsior. They stood in a bunch near the hot dog stand, talking loudly and milling about like restless cattle. (Oh, please God, let one of them ask me to dance the next dance.)

One of them — miraculously — did. And one of them asked my sister. Together with the fire warden's daughters in their hand-me-down clothes we went self-consciously to form a new square. ("Duck for the oyster, dip for the clam. All join hands and circle left.") During the slow waltz he told me that his name was Christopher Meyer and that he came from Gloversville. Was working "with these other clowns" at the YMCA camp on Lake Pleasant. His teeth stuck out a bit, but he was tall and brown and swung me way out and back, all my strength resting, trusting, on his arm. When quarter of eleven came it seemed like the end of the world. My sister had danced with several of the older boys, but I danced only with Chris. He said they were starting up square dances at the camp every Tuesday night, and I told him about Aunt Hettie. "We'll work something out," he said, and I believed him. (Our aunt received a visit from the director — the young man who had brought them in the camp pick-up truck — on behalf of the Young Men's *Christian* Association. There was nothing she could say, and my grandfather treated it all as a private joke.)

It turned out to be such a beautiful, beautiful summer. And innocent too, inspite of Aunt Hettie's forebodings. We danced every Tuesday and Saturday night, danced like two of the seven dancing princesses, and in the slow dances ("I touch your lips and all at once the flame grows high-yer/ I know I must surrender to your kiss of fi-yer?) we held each other around the waist and admitted, painfully, that we were in love. I gave him my sterling silver identification bracelet (bought on credit at Van Buren's Jewelers last Christmas and still not paid for) and he carved my name on a tree fungus at the top of T-Lake Mountain. I sent down to my mother for different coloured ribbons to thread through the eyelet on my petticoat and washed my hair every other day. On Chris's day off he and one of his pals would hitchhike over to see us, always terribly polite to Aunt Hettie — "Could we lift that down for you, Miss Goodenough?" — but *she* wasn't fooled, not a bit of it. She prayed for our immortal souls while we ate home-made brownies or played badminton doubles on the beach. Sometimes Chris and I would take out the boat with the double oars and row in contented unison over to the little island, where we wrote each other's names in the sand with a pointed stick, then ate tunafish sandwiches and drank Aunt Hettie's lemonade. Once I taped my initials on his back with adhesive tape, and five days later he pulled up his tee shirt to show me my brand, "I M C," white against the deepening brown of his back. I wore my nylon bathing suit, the colour of the setting sun. "You're lovely in that," he said, using the word, I think, for the very first time. We wrote daily letters back and forth, wrote "S W A K" across the seal. And yet content merely to touch — it seems incredible, no, unbelievable, to me now. Instead, he taught me to play the ukulele.

My father came home early from his travelling job in the South — we were never quite clear about why — and we had boxes of unsold seed packets around the house for years. He and my mother came up and my mother said of Chris, "What is he, German?" My sister went to the Poconos after all, but my twice weekly outings were so established by then that nobody sought to stop them.(Sometimes the hired man and I would exchange a look over a chicken leg or baking powder biscuit.) My mother and Aunt Hettie wrangled over the corn husks or potato peelings; my father fished on the lake or in the trout stream, wearing his brown rubber waders, at T-Lake Falls. My grandfather and Willie B. began chopping the wood for next year.

It didn't last beyond the summer — my love affair. His mother told him he had to return my bracelet by Labour Day, and I took it back, reluctantly. We exchanged school photographs and amateurish French kisses and promised we'd write every week. I can still see his brown, earnest face, his blue eyes (very like my grandpa's) as he said this. ("Oh, the moon shines tonight on Little Red Wing, her shoes are crackin', they need a blackin'.") The boys' camp had a final square dance and steak cookout. Chris and I sat a little apart and felt somewhat superior to the pretty but giggly girls from the summer cottages on Lake Constance and their joke-cracking, ham-fisted boyfriends. After dark we all went skinny-dipping in a lake turned as exciting and black and mysterious as the future. But did not even touch, this time, he and I — just sank into the dark water like two torches eager to be put out. We came out before the others and dried ourselves, backs turned, dressed and built up a huge fire for the singsong and marshmallow roast. ("There's a long, long trail a'windin'," "Green Grow the Rushes, O," "Oralee," "The Lonely Ash Grove.") I was late getting home and my mother gave me a lecture.

He never came back to the mountains. He wrote for a while and then stopped. I accepted this — that is to say I didn't try to telephone or threaten. He was killed in a car crash in November — the director told me eight months later. I doubt if his mother knew my last name.

I asked if I could have a new bathing suit.

"What's the matter with your old one? Surely you haven't grown that much?"

"I can't find it anywhere."

I had buried it, with the ukulele, in the deep sand beneath the boathouse. Aunt Hettie, if I had told her, would have probably said the whole thing was heavenly justice.

"Here," said my grandfather, staring at me intently with Christopher's blue eyes. "Buy yourself another."

I nodded and smiled at him. He knew. We bowed our heads. "For what we are about to receive, O Lord, make us truly thankful."

"I'll have a little of that there dressing, Mr. Goodenough, if you don't mind," said my father from the bottom of the table.

"Isobel! Come away from the windows."

"Mother, it's all right."

(Daddy was hiding in the back room, pretending to mark papers. Every time the lightning flashed I shuddered but stood still. Jane was downstairs with mother, trying to comfort the dog. The lightning wrote my name across the sky. There was a terrific thunderclap, as though a branch from the very Tree of Life had snapped. I longed to bury my face in a pillow but stood fast.)

Daddy came rushing out. "You'd better get away from the front of the house. Jesus!" He quickly pulled out the plug of the radio, jerked at it desperately and hurried back to safety. "You get away from there, you hear?"

When Aunt Caroline and Uncle Pudge were living here a ball of lightning rolled right out of the oven and up the kitchen wall. You never know.

"Isobel!"

Jane put her arms around the shaking dog.

"It's all right. It's all right. It's all right."

I opened the window and invited the lightning in.

Songs
of
Experience

twelve

Two things happened to me the summer I was seventeen: My grandfather sold his summer place and I went to work on the Hill. The second came about ultimately from the first, for it was because there was no more Journey's End that I had to spend my summer in the city for the first time in my (remembered) life. I couldn't believe it.

"Everything?"

"He's sold it all. Some retired couple from Amsterdam. You can bet your Aunt Hettie put him up to it."

Our father, muttering among the roses, declared to the neighbour's cat that it was a goddamned shame.

For me, it was like a cruel and unnecessary amputation, done in the night so that I woke up minus a vital limb, helpless, pain-racked, unable to believe in the empty sleeve, the sewn-up trouser leg.

"Why?"

"He says he can't afford it any more. He needs the money. Or that's what he says." Her mother gave a little snort. (And never offered it to us because he knew we had none.)

Like a legendary drowning man, I began to relive it all again. Looking back, I saw what seemed to be an endless succession of golden summers. Felt myself running again through pine and tamarack, running along the biscuit-coloured sand with Jane, running until the soles of our feet were on fire and then, still running, quenching our legs in the lake.

Rowing silently past the Knox's landing, looking for the bones of dead horses underneath their dock.

Netting minnows in the shallows.

The way we could rub the whitish bloom off blueberries and polish them with our fingertips.

The taste of wintergreen and wild strawberries.

The dusty-smelling buffalo rug in front of the huge stone fireplace, from the top of which Harry had fallen, like an outraged angel, just as he placed the last lot of motor around the very edge of the chimney. Down past the openmouthed hired man who stood on a ladder putting a lighted cigar into a wasps' nest under the eaves. (And survived, unhurt.)

The head of a deer shot by a silver bullet.

The rowing boat named *Jezobel* after me and Jane.

The Sears, Roebuck catalogues in the outhouse with their well-thumbed pages of men's and ladies' underwear and curious "hospital appliances" whose use we could not always figure out. One summer a huge roll of shiny toilet paper with pictures of Hitler, Mussolini, Hirohito: "Wipe Out the Axis." Now some asthmatic woman would lie under the orange afghan and stare wistfully at the clock above the mantelpiece, look through the stereopticon, admire the Northern Lights.

Her grandchildren would sleep in our bed.

"But I thought it would come to us!"

Clara, tight-lipped, her last dream dying hard.

"So did I, Isobel. So did I."

I cursed the fates that made Harry grow old and cautious, made my father a bad provider, made me seventeen and helpless. Through the dull brown fabric of our lives had run the golden thread of summer. I was terrified. Stifled. How could I live with these people, in this house?"

"It's no good crying, Isobel. What's done is done."

I refused to go and see Harry, who had betrayed me. Refused to make plans. Jane got a job as a counsellor at a summer camp in Maine. She was home from college for only a week, and then she went away again.

"It was getting unhealthy anyway. Just you and me and no social life."

"Shut up." She wrote letters to some boy in Ohio, in perfumed ink.

Aunt Olive gave me a string of cultured pearls for graduation, but no one invited me to the senior prom. Under my name in the yearbook, there were no activities listed. Just Isobel Marie Cleary and a touched-up photograph.

"Pretty girls are a dime a dozen," said Clara. "It's character that counts." And anyway I had won a scholarship (small consolation to us both).

The night of the senior prom I decided to kill myself, but didn't.

"Isobel, have you made any plans for the summer?"

"Leave me alone."

"Why don't you ask Mrs. Cooper if she wants you to baby sit?"

"Mrs. Cooper has gone to Lake George."

"Maybe you should take a typing course. We might be able to swing it."

"That would be a great way to spend the summer, wouldn't it?"

Aunt Hettie came up with some chicken soup and I slammed the door in her face.

I went down to the New York State employment agency, where I was offered a job demonstrating hairbrushes in a department store.

I tried the *Press* and the *Sun*.

"We don't need any new reporters, but we could use an office girl. How fast do you type?"

The Presbyterian church: "Except for our secretary all the addressing and bulletin work is volunteer. Now, if you'd like to help out in the summer Sunday school...."

Someone had been married the day before; there was confetti in the gutters.

Most of the kids I knew at Central High had summer jobs which they had been holding down since they were fifteen or so, if they were working at all. A lot were away at their summer cottages. I decided, at last, that I would begin my novel and be famous by the middle of my freshman year. I lay on my bed staring aimlessly at the same piece of yellow paper, listening to the radio and trying not to listen to my parents quarrelling with each other about my lack of ambition, my unpopularity, my "unhealthy" attitude toward Journey's End. After four days I gave up what was essentially a pretence anyway ("Are you going to let anybody see what you've written, honey?") and just lay about in my bathing suit in the backyard, reading.

My father, like Mr. MacGregor, hoed his tiny vegetable patch and weeded around his roses, talking to himself. He, too, was lost without his summers. He looked at me sometimes but never saw me; his eyes were full of brooks and leaping trout.

My mother stayed inside, mostly, cooking the elaborate meals he demanded, even in the summertime. Sometimes she would come out on the pack porch and we would shuck peas together (later corn), but there was tension, not peace, between us. It was not simply because I didn't have a job. I had not been brought up to think that I should contribute to my room and board, although, considering our always precarious financial position, I should have done just that. It was more to do with her own troublesome relationship with my father, to which I was now the sole and reluctant witness, and her despair that in spite of all her sacrifices, her doing without, her letters, her phone calls, her own self-abnegation, I had not turned out the way I should. The laughing golden-haired baby of her snapshots had turned into a proud, sullen, ungrateful, solitary creature. There had been no talk of a summer job this year until my grandfather sold the cabin. If I had been running off to State

Park or Ansco Lake with a group of teenagers she would have warned me about drinking and losing my reputation and worried until I was safely home again, but she would not have been so desperately ashamed (and therefore angry) at my continued presence in the house. It began to dawn on her that I would never be the golden girl she had dreamed of but simply Isobel, her daughter, another of life's misfits. I was a fact, I was there, *all the time*, apparently friendless, ambitionless — at least in so far as the summer was concerned — adopting arrogant postures and rarely deigning to "lift so much as a finger" to help her with the housework.

So there was my father, in an old straw hat to protect him against the sun, muttering among the vegetables and flowers. And there was my mother, her hair coming away from its pins, her eyes angry and baffled behind the thick bifocals she was forced to wear, weeping over the ironing and the apple pies or lying across her bed in the heat of the afternoon, reading her endless ladies' magazines. Dust stood ankle-thick beneath the beds, and the flies came in through the hole in the kitchen door.

I lay on my stomach under the apple tree, reading *The Atlantic Monthly* and *True Confessions*, watching the ants or just daydreaming, wishing something, anything, would happen to relieve the utter boredom of my life. An earthquake or a lover: It really was irrelevant what so long as it was something. To make things worse we were experiencing a heat wave and at night the air was full of sheet lightning and barking dogs, of other people's radios and other people's fights, the cloying smell of petunias and phlox and summer flowers dying from the sun. Not changing my horizontal posture of the daytime, I would lie at night on the other twin bed in my sister's room (her bed strangely prim and flat, as though there had been a sudden death in the family), sheetless and sweating, unable to keep still, my mind and body connected to the nervous flicker of the skies.

Some nights my father would ask me to ride down with him to Cherka's Ice Cream, the only place left, according to him, where you could still get decent hand-packed ice cream. I always stayed in the car, the rough pile of the seats unbearable against my naked legs, while he went in. Couples went by, their arms around each other, on the way back from the last show at the Capitol or Strand. Groups of boys in convertibles or cars with cut-out mufflers cruised around looking for groups of girls or "action." I would slide down in my seat for fear of being recognized with my father. Car radios played "Kiss of Fire" and "Love Letters in the Sand." Requested by Betty Lou for Dick Remember When. An earthquake or a lover — preferably both.

When my father came out after chatting for a while with the girl behind the big cardboard tubs of ice cream ("Hot enough for you? Say, d'you think it's gonna rain?") we drove home slowly and cautiously, he cursing the other drivers and braking at every possible opportunity, the cold white ice cream carton between my legs, my mother's inevitable pineapple Dixie cup in my hand, the little wooden spoon, like a tongue depresser, done up in its wrapper. Then he and she should sit on the porch and eat and wait until they got sleepy enough to think of going to their separate beds. I would hear my father on the porch below, clearing his throat or striking one last match for one last cigarette. Or talking to our old cocker spaniel, kneeling down to scratch her behind the ears: "She's a hot old girlie-wirlie."

Then he would come in and latch the screen door, go out in the kitchen to sniff for gas and go heavily upstairs to bed.

My sister sent postcards of covered bridges and pine trees: "Having a wonderful time." The tar on the streets softened and bubbled and the little kids on the block took twigs and poked away happily at the gooey, fragrant stuff.

("Allie, Allie in free, Allie, Allie in free."

"Louise! Dougie! It's time to go to bed.")

A dead cat lay squashed in the middle of Riverside Drive until somebody kicked it over to the side. The last of the June roses drooped on the dining room table.

I longed for my grandfather's woods, the cool mountain nights, the belching frogs, the liquid embrace of the lake.

("Is it hot enough for you?"

"Have you ever *seen* such a summer?")

In the second week of the heat wave my mother refused to cook any more and my father brought home cartons of macaroni and potato salads and beige packages of cold cuts from the deli-catessen. I found that even the sound of their chewing was enough to drive me into cramps of rage. I stuck my nails into my palms until they bled. It seemed incredible to me that I wouldn't murder one or both of them before the summer was out.

("Is there any more of that potato salad, Muddie?" We ate right out of the cartons, only stopping to set out the cold cuts on a plate.

"You've got a bit of egg on your cheek."

"Where?"

"On your left cheek. Take it off. Quick. It makes me sick to look at it."

"Is it off?"

"No. You missed it. Here.")

I went back downtown to the employment office to see if the hairbrush job was still available. Maybe, I thought, Rapunzel-like, that some prince would just happen into the department store and be struck by the vision of me brushing out my long, long hair.

It wasn't.

"It's too bad you can't type, dear. We could certainly place a typist."

"Look, isn't there anything, *anything* I could do?"

She looked up at me where I stood, desperate, in front of her desk. A tired-looking woman of advancing middle age whose upper arms had run to fat. She frowned and studied me carefully, then took a card from her index file.

"D'you think your parents would let you work at the state hospital?"

"You mean the *mental* hospital?"

"Yes. They're asking for a female aide."

My first impulse was to turn and walk straight out of there. In many ways my upbringing had been as sheltered as that of a girl in a convent. It came to me that I knew nothing of the town outside of downtown, the department stores and specialty shops, the banks and credit offices, the Presbyterian church, the library, the movie houses and a bit of the West Side.

When I gave him my dime I had always turned my head away from the blind pencil seller at the corner of Main and Chenango streets. I had never seen a dead person, let alone a mad one. In my reading, yes — but those people, however real for a moment, were like the shadow people of Plato's cave. Like them, they had only an imaginary reality. A distant cousin had committed suicide by sticking her head in an oven — something to do with a man. Aunt Hettie had drunk iodine and stood shaking and determined on a window ledge. Leslie's father had cut himself open with a razor. There was an old man, at Halloween, who was rumoured to put bits of broken glass and razor blades in apples and an old woman who rocked and sang and called out to us from her porch on the way to school. But all this was either long ago or far away or pretty well removed from any direct contact with myself.

"I don't think ..." I began.

("Life!" said a sudden sharp voice in my ear. "Life, Isobel!" And then, in a softer tone, "Money.")

"I'll take it."

"You'll have to see the director tomorrow morning" and gave me directions for the bus and warned me about comfortable shoes.

I walked back toward the Front Street bridge in a daze. It seemed to me — perhaps I hoped — that my parents would never allow it.

"Germs, Isobel! You never know what you might...."

And what would the neighbours say?

I had just committed the first truly independent act of my life and I was scared. I looked at the shop fronts and the houses as though I were seeing them for the first time. Freedom had never seemed so sweet, summer so inviting. There was still time to change my mind. I stood in the middle of the bridge, leaning on the parapet and gazing down into the muddy river. What did I

136

expect to see reflected there? My face? A sign? There was only a metallic shimmer, painful to look at, where the sun spread itself on the water. I walked on while overhead, as if to mock me, a crayon-yellow airplane completed a capitol "I," like God beginning my name in the summer sky.

I still hadn't told them by nighttime. Did I want them to say yes or no? They could stop me if they wanted to. I was still, legally, their possession, an extension of themselves.

They sat on the porch, each locked in the silence of their own unhappiness; the sexless old dog lay on her side between them. I offered to go for some ginger-ale and fled down the sweating street. I walked and walked, up one familiar street and down another, the paper bag under my arm. I had bought some crullers as well, for I knew my parents liked them. Along Riverside Drive with its substantial-looking houses set well back from the street, the blue light of a television set occasionally glimpsed through a side window, but many of them dark, their owners fled to the lake to spend the summer. A stranger, leading an enormous Afghan hound, passed me going in the opposite direction. I turned up Millard and then back up Bennett Hill. Sprinklers were still on and somewhere over on the next street I could hear the thin, utterly helpless cry of a baby made desolate by the heat. Right now, at the cabin, I thought, I would be lying in my private little circle of warmth listening to the chipmunks on the roof, the pine trees rubbing against the window.

"This time last year ..." It was a game I'd played since I was very small. However chaotic the personal relationships within our family there had been a preciseness to my days and to my turnings. Now I was about to break that pattern, and the heavy, restless night, the unknown baby's cry, seemed ominous and foreboding.

"Listen," I said to my parents, who were still sitting on the porch. "I've taken a job. I'm going to work on the Hill."

Then I went inside to find us some glasses and an opener.

"Knock, knock."
"Who's there?"
"Isobel."
"Isobel who?"
"Is a bell necessary on a bicycle?"

thirteen

Sometimes I wonder now if I did it all, initially, just for the satisfaction of slamming the screen door behind me and listening, from the kitchen, to their shocked silence. Or did I, out of an inner desperation, take desperate measures to try and insure that if I couldn't have Journey's End, my Eden, I would sample the fruits of hell? Thinking back, I am surprised as well that they ever let me go. They had both been in hospital. Perhaps they saw an aide as one of the pert candy stripers who plumped pillows and arranged flowers and came around twice a day to ask if you'd like grape juice or ginger-ale. Perhaps, too, they simply did not know what to do with me, or what other alternatives to offer. I slept very well that night, much to my surprise, and woke up refreshed, albeit frightened. Sometimes any decision is better than no decision at all.

I took the familiar St. John Avenue bus downtown and then transferred to the Robinson Street bus. The route ran parallel but somewhat above the railway tracks and stopped finally at the foot of State Hospital Hill, where I was supposed to get a shuttle bus to the hospital itself. I got off and stood there, rather forlorn in my old ballerina skirt and ballet slippers and my lunch done up in a paper bag. Then I noticed a lot of white-clad and blue-clad figures standing across the street, so I followed them, handed in my transfer when the bus finally came and sat with my eyes on my lap. The voices around me were loud and hard and jocular, like the voices of the vocational school boys who hung out in the basement of the high school and made obscene remarks to the girls as they went into the cafeteria. I had no idea where to go when I got off the bus and took refuge with two nondescript old women, cleaning ladies probably, who pointed out the way to the main building, a large oblong box of yellow stucco, about six stories high — a long sand-coloured rectangle. It might have been made at some gigantic seaside with a box instead of a pail, it was so smooth and regular in design. But the windows, one above the other in six neat rows, were barred and screened — hardly a child's idea of a castle. A long semicircular drive led up to and away from the main entrance, and over to the side was a small parking area marked DOCTORS ONLY. There were signs saying HOSPITAL but no signs saying QUIET.

I stood outside, uncertain, looking at my graduation watch.

7:57

("Isobel, you are dying faster than the day.")

Two men in white uniforms, like dentists, walked past on rubber-soled shoes. They ignored me completely, great bunches of keys jangling in their pockets, and disappeared into the building. I followed a cautious distance behind and watched as one of them selected a small key and stuck it in a plaque on the wall where the elevator buttons should have been. A light went on and the indicator over the door swung downward like a pendulum toward "M." I think that if they had said one word to me I would have run like mad through the door and sought the sunshine. But they didn't, and as I stood there in the hall, wondering what to do next, I said to myself, in my head, "Last year at this time the fire would already be burning off the chill and we would all be around the table eating pancakes and maple syrup. Mist would be rising from the lake like steam from a cup of coffee. Those goddamned beavers have flooded the creek again."

The two men, laughing and never even glancing in my direction — I could have been Invisible Scarlett O'Neill — got in the elevator, using another small key to open the heavy door, and I was left alone. As the door shut a sentence was cut off and dangled, unfinished, in the corridor.

"We had to ream him twice before...."

It made no sense. I was alone in the hall with an incomplete thought. No one came or went; the indicator above the near elevator would remain forever fixed at "5." The silence was final. The silence was terrible.

Then the indicator on the other elevator started down. That's what gave me the courage, in the end, to move. I didn't want to be caught or confronted by whatever might come out. I looked around me, blinking, like Alice down the rabbit hole. Down the left-hand corridor, just a little ways from the elevator, was a small neon sign that had not yet been switched off from the night. DIRECTOR. Another dentist was inside, asleep with his head on his arms. No one had seen me. I could still go home. The director was asleep. ("Last year at this time I was putting out the leftover pancakes for the coons. The mist rises like steam from a cup of coffee. My bare feet are cold on the forest path.") I knocked.

He sat up, blinking at me through thick spectacles, said "yes?" as though he couldn't believe his eyes. And then he woke up to who I was.

"Come in. Come in. You must be the new aide. Sorry." He took off his glasses, polished them on his smock and put them on again. We had a ten minute interview in which he insisted I call him "Mike" while he fussed, as he talked, with a big metal spindle on which were caught, like so many butterflies, little pastel memorandum slips. In the corner was an American flag on a flag stand and on the wall behind the desk was a picture of President Eisenhower. In fact, the office was not very different from a principal's office: the flag, the picture, the same dully varnished straightbacked chairs along one wall, the same huge timetable, the same air of preoccupation with telephone calls and papers. Even the rows of keys, hanging on a pegboard, were not alien to the image of a principal. But the dentist's get-up and the fruit boots, as we called them then, made him look out of place, not me. I wondered if I would have to wear a uniform too. The idea was not unpleasant.

He wanted me to feel free to come to him at any time. He wanted to know how old I was and if I had any disabilities. He wanted to know, by golly, if I was Warren Cleary's daughter and my gosh I went to school with your dad over thirty years ago. He wanted to know where the time had gone. He pressed a button and stood up, began taking some keys off the pegboard.

"I think we'll put you on eighty-eight, Isobel. They could do with some extra help because their PN is on sick leave."

"Eighty-eight."

"Yes. The girls in charge of that ward are two of the best we have. You should get along just fine. Mind you, we may have to shift you around from time to time."

"Shift me around."

He nodded. "Relief work. Somebody gets sick. Somebody goes on vacation. You know how it is." I didn't.

A woman stuck her head around the door.

"You want me, Mike?"

"Yeah. Will you take Isobel up to eighty-eight and introduce her to the ward? Tell Gert to be good to her. I know her dad." He slid my keys onto a metal ring and fitted all this on a lanyard.

"It's best to wear them around your waist at all times. And for heaven's sake don't lose them." He gave me a fatherly pat on the head as we moved out toward the elevators. The woman, whom I took to be a secretary of some sort, showed me which keys to use. We got in the elevator; she pressed the "4" button and regarded me with frank curiosity.

"What are you, a med student or something?" I just shook my head, afraid that if I said anything I might start to cry. The elevator seemed cramped and utterly devoid of air, and I could smell the woman's powder and too sweet toilet water. ("The pine needles leave a scent on your hands, Isobel — the moss, the secret, private smell of fungus and wild mushrooms. The sun rises higher. It is time to put up the flag on its long, long pole.")

I spoke, surprising myself. "I want the money."

It sounded very callous and was only partly true; but the woman nodded, satisfied. It seemed an adequate reason. The elevator stopped and we got off. She led me up the hall to a windowless door marked 88 in big black numbers and knocked. Nothing happened, so she knocked again.

"Probably thinks I'm one of the boys from Albany," she said, "and is doing up her face." Then we heard the sound of a key (no footsteps — "The door must be soundproofed," I thought) and the door swung out. The woman who appeared before us was very tall and thin, with two hectic disks of colour on her cheeks. She wore glasses with butterfly frames.

"Hello, Stella. What do you have for us today? Visitors?" She flashed me a professional but not unkindly smile.

"A present from the boss. This here's Isobel. Your new relief." She gave me a little shove and I found myself on the other side of the door. The nurse shut the door with a bang and locked it.

"Welcome to the shit ward," she said.

We were in another long corridor, and beyond, in a big room, lay such a tangle of noise and smell that I drew back in terror, pulling away from her arm. I was right on the edge of some vast cliff — all my instincts told me to turn and run. ("Last year I was. Last year I. Last year.") That there was still time; that I never should have come here at all; that I would find some other way to learn about humanity, about *Life*, than this deliberate dive into such stench and sound as were coming from that room.

"You won't believe this," she said, her flippant manner gone, "but we don't even notice it any more." She took my arm again and I allowed myself to be led along, past side wards containing glimpses of bare flesh and solitary madness ("A trout jumped over by Knox's place. For pleasure, maybe, or seeking a fly. I'll take a boat out this morning and just drift") all those who couldn't measure up to the standards of the ward. My curiosity had fled and I tried to keep my eyes unseeing.

"Here they are," she said, with an ironic sweep of her hand. "Not exactly ready for the President's garden party, are they?"

I took a deep breath and stared. Four rows of iron bedsteads. In each bed, sitting up or lying down, was an old woman in a coarse hospital gown. Another nurse was at the far end, doing something I couldn't make out. Nearly all of the women were talking, some just in mutters, some in words, some in curses and screams. One enormous fat woman was rolling up balls of something and throwing them at the wall. I saw old naked ladies with grey pubic hair, white pubic hair, streaks of brown excrement on their faces and legs (I knew what that woman was rolling), toothless faces, ancient glittering eyes.

"Hello, darling," the fat woman called. "Hello." I had not known that madness would stink or speak to me directly. I felt that I would vomit if I didn't faint first. The fat woman raised her arm to a throwing position.

"That's right," she said. "That's all right, darling. That's lovely."

"Mrs. Kolodzy," I said, "I can't work here."

("By this time the sun has burnt away the mist. Far enough out I ship the oars and let the water take me where it will. I shut my eyes.")

She pulled a chair out of the nurses' station.

"Sit down and put your head down," she said, pressing me into the chair. The floor beneath my head rocked dangerously. (An earthquake or a lover. Last year I ...)

Two weeks later I pick up a ball of shit and toss it back to Sophie, who laughs hugely at my joke and promptly puts it in her mouth and eats it. Two weeks later I know what reaming is and wear my keys on a long rope around my waist. I have seen a woman drink from a bedpan and another, in a crêpe-paper nightie, sent to a pauper's grave.

And thus did I lose my mind's virginity.

fourteen

By the time I went home the first night I had resolved to quit. I soaked in the bath for an hour, washed my hair and my clothes, but still the smell remained. I couldn't eat my dinner.

"What's the matter, Isobel?"

"It's nothing. It's the heat."

My father helped himself to another piece of layer cake. I asked to be excused and turned on the bathroom tap loud so no one could hear me throwing up.

By the third day I knew I had made it. It was partly a matter of pride (always before, when something had not gone just as I wanted it, my mother had allowed, indeed suggested, that I quit), partly the sense that at last I was being tested as a human being. The work was hard and very physical but mentally exhausting as well. And yet. And yet. In many ways it was easier for me to cope with the avowed madness of Ward 88 than the glossed-over violence of my home. If I had said to my mother, "You're crazy," she would have been shocked, horrified, cut to the quick and then furious.

If I said it to Sophie (which I didn't), she would have answered, "Hello. Lovely. Yes."

The terrible strain of all those years of pretending we were a "normal" family had taken a terrible toll on me. Those crazy ladies, who were known by everybody, including themselves, to be mad, were refreshing. Once I got over my physical repugnance, I began, if not to enjoy myself, at least to relax. I still went to Cherka's with my father for ice cream, still lay on my bed thinking about love or being a writer, still missed the woods with a terrible, unbelievable ache. But gradually, as the summer wore on, my past life and my time at home took on more and more the character of a dream or some of the old, faded, slightly out-of-focus snapshots in one of my mother's innumerable candy boxes. My "real" life was only what happened on the Hill. Each day now I took a shower and washed my hair before I left work and changed into a clean skirt and blouse. Put my keys and cap in my bag just as soon as I left the building. So that the "me" who took the bus back downtown twenty minutes later had nothing to do with the "me" who had a life on 88. Damp-haired and dusted with talcum powder, I could have been any kid coming back from a day at State Park or Ouaquaga Lake. That part became a kind of game. At first I stayed on to spite the Fates. Later I stayed on because it became impossible for me to leave. Like a gambler who is too far into the game to quit, I determined to play the summer to its end. A year later I would read the lines "After the first death / There is no other." My attitude to what I saw and did during those days was exactly that. After the first morning it was never so bad again.

I worked seven to three-thirty six days a week with the seventh off, so there was never any two-day stretch of the nothingness at home to cope with. When I did have a day off I slept late, read and sunbathed the rest of the day or went down to Joseph's to try on smart, expensive clothes for fall. Nobody suggested I should contribute a penny to the household.

("Isn't she just adorable? Esther, Annalee, have you ever seen anything so cute?" I allowed them to pin and tuck me, show me outfits for fraternity parties and proms, Bermuda shorts and knee socks. "What are you doing this summer, dear?" Congratulating me on my scholarship. They had seen in the paper.... "Esther, bring in the new Lanz for Isobel. It's made for her." Plump, sleek sales-ladies with hearts of gold and mouths full of steel dress-maker's pins. "Turn around, darling, and look at yourself in the mirror.")

All the other days I got up at six, made breakfast for myself and my father, whose asthma had made him an erratic sleeper. Then took a bus downtown, where I transferred to the Robinson Street bus. It's funny, for I was never close to my father and we never once had a genuine conversation, a strip-ping away of layers; but I remember those early-morning sum-mer breakfasts as really pleasant times. He would put the coffee on to perk and I would make scrambled eggs. Sometimes we had sliced tomatoes from the garden, yellow or red, still with the spicy smell of the tomato vines about them. Occasionally a grapefruit or a melon. One day he said to me, "Say, d'you remember when you kids both had the measles and I brought you up a grapefruit with a maraschino cherry on it every day?" I said I remembered and he said, "Yeah. Jesus. Where does the time go?" This was the closest we ever got to philosophy.

There were always a few of his rather blowsy roses in a glass bowl on the dining room table, and the smell of cut grass and flowers drifted in through the window screens. We never talked about my job after the first day when I told him the director knew him years ago. This pleased him, for he had an almost pathetic desire to be "remembered" or "known." But he also had an absolute terror of death or disease or deviation from the norm (which is why I think my mother's accusations about that long-ago high school lavatory were probably groundless). I knew — and counted on this — that he would never "drop up" to see this man one morning, although he pretended he might. The gardening had tanned his arms as far up as the short-sleeve sport shirts he always wore, and his face and neck were freckled and pinky-brown. At fifty-five his face was still round and boyish, and he had a round body like the stereotype of the school fat boy. He ate like a boy too, head down and earnestly, forking the pale yellow egg into his eager mouth. I knew I could ruin his pleasure with one or two stories, like well-placed kicks. Supposing I described the huge tins of powered scrambled egg that the night staff would be dipping into just about now — mixing it with water as though it were poster paint, which it might just as well have been considering the use some of the ladies put it to. Or what some of the patients mixed with their breakfast egg. Or how everything had to be chopped and mashed, with the exception of toast or cookies, for easy feeding and easier digestion. No-colour, no-texture pap to keep our crazy babies going.

Suppose I demonstrated how to force-feed a recalcitrant patient or described what the bedding would be like by the time I got there. Or reaming. But I never did. Was this because, in the end, I loved him? Instead I picked up my dishes and carried them into the kitchen, to add to the dishes from the night before. Then I collected my cap and keys and extra outfit (my father usually avoided looking at the keys directly, got out the dog food or poured himself another cup of coffee) and went on my way.

I wore old dirndl skirts and sneakers or ballet slippers, Mrs. Kolodzy having persuaded the director that it was silly and too expensive for me to buy the drab slate-blue orderly's uniform for just six weeks of wear. This meant, ironically enough, that while I could pass for an old teenager on the bus I stood out rather badly once I got to the Hill. During the course of the summer I was mistaken for an ambulatory patient more than once, particularly if I was with Mrs. Kolodzy or Mrs. Reynolds, who wore stiff white uniforms all the time. (In fact, I can't imagine them in any other garb.)

Once off the shuttle bus, filled with men in white suits and women in white or blue, a few cleaning ladies with red hands and old felt slippers in their handbags, I hurried toward my unreal world again. I still didn't trust the rest of the hospital and the smart remarks of the male nurses embarrassed and frightened me as a group of us waited in the silent, soundproof hall for an elevator to come down. They knew who I was — the gossip on the wards was virtually all interhospital scandal and romance — and also sensed that I was "different." Most of the staff came from the East Side and the First Ward around Clinton Street, poor Irish or Slavs — tough in mind and body, with muscular upper arms beneath their short-sleeved smocks. They gave off an aura of power and sex and self-confidence. Would talk about me as though I couldn't hear.

"How's that for a nice piece of ass?" "Accidentally" pressing against me in the elevator and laughing if I flinched of moved away.

"Oh. Sorry." Winking at one another.

Mrs. Reynolds warned me about them — "chickenshit punks." "Sweetheart, they'll knock you up and leave you when you begin to show. Stay away from them." She was divorced and very cynical about men; so was Mrs. Kolodzy. If I went over to the dining hall with one or the other the men would call out from the porch where they were sitting and waiting out the lunch hour, "Hey, Florence, lend us the princess for a quick fuck," and the nurses would reply, possessively, "She's not for you wiseacres. Leave her alone." I could feel their cool eyes appraising me as we walked into the hall to get our trays and stand in line for heavy, high-protein dinners of shepherd's pie or beef stew, ladled out by two deaf mutes. Cottage pudding for dessert. Lemon meringue pie. "Eat up, dearie, you'll need it. We're cutting fingernails and toenails after lunch." I played with my food and wondered what it would really be like to go out with one of those men.

So that once out of the elevator (sometimes they threatened not to let me out, put a key in "Hold" and stood there, smiling) I hurried toward the safety of the ward. The night nurse and her helper, an elderly, fat, bad-tempered PN, were just finishing up the breakfasts. Two trusties were pushing the steam table along the hall, and there was a smell of urine and shit and coffee in the air. Mrs. Kolodzy, who was very conscientious, was always there ahead of me, and Mrs. Reynolds would arrive a few minutes after.

"Anybody die?"

"Nope."

"Well, there's always tonight, bless their little hearts."

We sat in the tiny staff lounge, midway between the big ward and the little "side wards" which were really only single rooms. Drinking coffee and waiting for the night staff to leave. The room was full of confession and romance magazines, old *Reader's Digests*, overstuffed sofas and chairs. The PN was putting "her" mug (initials painted on with nail polish) back on the shelf above the sink, sighing. She didn't like Mrs. Kolodzy or Mrs. Reynolds or — by extension — me. I think she felt that the day staff ought to get there in time to help with the breakfasts. There we were, chatting, while she ... Terribly overweight and with the sour breath of the chronically angry. She kept her spare belongings in an old bowling bag.

"It's all very well," proclaimed her outraged back. "It's all very well for *some* people." Mrs. Kolodzy went to check the night nurses' report. Mrs. Reynolds pulled up her skirt and adjusted a garter and then our day really began.

The three of us, together with our one ambulatory patient, a Negro lady Mrs. Reynolds called Black Mumble but whose real name was Cora Lee, began to clean the ward. Cora Lee didn't seem to like me very much — I think she believed I was a trusty as well and would take away the little perks she got from the two nurses, so Mrs. Reynolds and I usually began together, Mrs. Kolodzy and Cora Lee following behind. It was such a strange, back-breaking and ludicrous business, this restoration of order, that we all (except Cora) fell into a kind of manic humour, singing and talking to our ladies, making jokes. There was a voluptuous sense of "letting go," of playing at what they did for real, so that the work went fairly quickly. Beginning with the first bed, which belonged to a very old lady named Agnes, we would roll the patient over to the very edge, whip off the soiled sheets — undersheet, mackintosh sheet, draw sheet — and make up exactly half the bed. Then we would zoom the old dear over to the other side and quickly unroll and tuck in the rest of the bedding. One develops a certain rhythm doing this and a certain speed. Some of the ladies would screech and claw at us, afraid they would roll right off the edge of the bed. But this never happened — they fell, but it was not of our doing — and their cries would be greeted by our laughter. Little clawlike hands with horny yellow nails. I can still feel them clutching me like monkey's paws. Great heaps of soiled linen piled up in the middle of the aisles. When we were finished it would be dumped into big canvas duffel bags with "88" stencilled on them and shoved down a long chute to the laundry in the basement of the building — a place I visited once, positively hellish with its heat and steam and slow grey-clothed figures shuffling to and fro.

The worst of the excrement would be rubbed off the body with the old sheet and we would wrap her in a big coarse towel. Then the second pair would come along with a trolley containing buckets of water, soap, more towels, huge diapers which tied (no pins allowed), a hairbrush, swabs, cornstarch and Gentian Violet. I, who had rarely seen my mother naked, and *never* any other lady (when Auntie O. came to visit, if you so much as approached the bathroom she called out in a frightened voice, "What is it? Who's there? Is that you, Clara?" or "Somebody's in here!" as though she were in a strange hotel), saw and scrubbed every inch of these old mad women with their wrinkled breasts, collapsed bellies and stinking bedsores. It was an incredible leap for the mind to make, and I'm not sure that I made it, then or ever. Scratching at their genitals with little dry mousy sounds, like fingers desperately searching for the one string that will release a perfect note.

"Watch," said Mrs. Reynolds. She began stroking the woman we were working on. Stroking her very gently, just using one finger, pushing the old, withered, desperate arm away with her elbow. I stood there transfixed (With what? Shame? Sadness? Curiosity? Perhaps a little of each).

"Watch Louella do her stunt." The long, sure finger of Mrs. Reynolds moved faster, explored inner folds and petals, released secret springs of pleasure. The old woman clamped her shrivelled legs tight over the nurse's working hand. And began to moan, to give little doglike yips of pleasure. And then cried out, "Yes, O, God, O yes harder harder Jesus Jesus Jeeeee ..." Hands pulling at useless breasts, eyes shut, toothless mouth pulled back in a terrible grin.

"Do it to me!"

Mrs. Kolodzy and Cora Lee had come up to watch.

"That's right, darling," called Sophie. "That's the way." There was a violent spasm and the creature lay quiet, gasping like a fish.

"It's the only time she ever says an intelligible word," said Mrs. Reynolds, peeling off her glove. The four of us moved on to the next bed.

Some of the women had skin so rotten and full of holes that we held handkerchiefs soaked in Old Spice cologne to our faces as we worked. The nurses gouged and painted, peering down into craters of unimaginable pain. Sometimes we could see right down to the bone, which glistened like mother-of-pearl or abalone, as though, in reward for such a life, the women were suffering a strange and beautiful sea change, as in Ariel's song. Meanwhile the mad thing under their grasp wriggled and screamed and cursed us with unholy cursing.

I scraped shit off the beds with an old table knife, mopped floors slippery with urine or vomit. Braided the hair of the little Ukrainian woman, red-cheeked and totally mad, whom they had nicknamed "Toot-Toot" because this was all she said. Avoided Sophie's shit balls. Changed the sanitary pads on Judith, the only youngish woman on the general ward, a woman with blank eyes and long, luxuriant blue-black hair. She had tried a leap from a high bridge and survived but was paralyzed from the waist down.

Her husband and mother would come to see her on visiting day.

"Here we are again, Judy."

"She looks well, doesn't she?"

"Very well."

"We brought you a nice nightie. Look here, darling, at the nightie. Blue. Your favourite." (Trying not to see the other women, trying to pretend this is just an ordinary hospital ward. Avoiding, by mutual unspoken consent, the eyes of the other visitors.)

"Won't you talk to us today, darling?"

("Hello, darling," calls Sophie, done up in a restraining jacket for visitors' day. "Hello.")

"Is there anything you'd like?" Bringing flowers which would be left to wilt in five-pound mayonnaise jars in the sunroom. Judith lies with her eyes shut, utterly motionless. Only her beautiful black hair alive and glistening. Suddenly she thrusts her arm underneath the sheet, comes up with a bloodied hand.

"Fuck off."

They leave, the mother sobbing into her handkerchief.

"I don't know," she says to Mrs. Kolodzy. "Why was she spared for this?"

Mrs. Kolodzy murmurs something noncommittal, walks them to the locked door and lets them out.

Judith lies smiling in her sleep.

Lunch takes nearly an hour. Those who can't or will not eat at all are fed, some forcibly. Plastic plates and enamel drinking cups with spouts. Milky tea runs down into the folds of their necks. Clean nightgowns are covered in mashed Spam and mashed potato. Sophie eats with relish, sitting straight up in bed, feeding herself.

"Lovely. Oh, lovely."

Toot-Toot carefully makes a well in her mashed potato and fills it up with tea.

Afterward we take turns going out for lunch. How *can* I be hungry, but I am. Sometimes we drive in Mrs. Reynold's convertible to the Dairy Queen, where we buy sundaes-to-go and return to the ward, where we all eat together in the staff room. Sometimes to the dining hall, walking across lawns worthy of an Ivy League college, an expensive resort. The sunlight makes me blink.

("Hey Florence. Lend us the princess for a quick fuck.")

Occasionally stopping at the hospital store, where salesmen from cigarette companies force free samples on us. A line of patients who have been in shock are seated at the counter drinking sodas. I wonder what it feels like to ...?

"Sweetheart, they don't feel a thing."

Back to the ward to make swabs, sitting with our feet up, chatting, a heap of cotton wool and packages of sticks on the table in front of us. The crazy ladies nap and mutter. The shades shut the sunlight out. Mrs. Kolodzy begins to write up her report.

"I don't think Aggie will last more than a few days."

"I've never seen a dead person."

"Never?"

"Nope." Winding the cotton wool tight with my thumb and index finger.

"We'll have to see what we can do."

Ward 88. The Shit Ward.

And outside, down in the town, the golden girls strolled back and forth in their summer dresses.

fifteen

The side wards on 88 were reserved for those who were too disturbed or disturbing, too mad or bad to be thrown into the general stew of the open ward. There were five of these little rooms, spaced along one side of the long hall which led from the nurses' station to the big locked door. Rooms within a room — like Chinese boxes and like a circus side show, they contained the most bizarre specimens — at least by someone's definition.

While I was on 88 only three of the wards were occupied, the first by an old woman who was cataleptic, and who stood for hours and would have stood forever, I think, if she hadn't been arbitrarily moved every so often by the nurses. In one position, arm high and forward in a kind of Nazi salute. Her skinny, shrivelled legs never trembled; her eyes never blinked. More witch than woman, more skeleton than witch. She was always dressed in a long hospital nightgown, got from one of the men's wards, I expect, and if the day was cool Mrs. Kolodzy or Mrs. Reynolds would wrap a blanket around her where she stood. Of all the old ladies she was the most removed and hence the most terrifying. I would stand at the open door of her room and return her stare, but I felt she could see right through me, right to the very core where all my shameful thoughts, desires and aspirations were hid. Once I went very, very close to her, in spite of my fear and her stink, and saw my face reflected in her eyes. Where was she? Why had this strange thing happened to her and not to me? I felt that if I really let myself go I could fall right into her, become her, know what it was like to be truly astonished, turned to stone. But no. I shook myself violently, like someone trying to wake up from a dream he knows he is dreaming and fled her upraised blessing or her curse. Had she spoken would she, like the Ancient Mariner, have held me transfixed with tales of nightmare ships and the woman Death-in-Life? I went back to the safety of the ward.

The second room was occupied by an old lady who was a typhoid carrier. Her door was kept shut all day, but I could peer in and see her walking back and forth, muttering to herself, or building little mouse nests, tearing up the funny papers she liked to read. At mealtimes whoever was feeding her put on surgical gown and cap, a surgical mask and gloves. She opened the door and held out her hands for milky tea, creamed chipped beef, mashed potatoes, custard. All the time chattering at us O dear O dear O my yes, like Tabitha Twitchit. Afterward her dishes were dropped in a special bag and taken away to be sterilized. Isolated by madness, isolated by carrying within herself the destruction of other people. Rooms within rooms. Nowadays, I suppose, they would simply have taken her gall bladder out. Then, at least, she would have the companionship of the other doomed souls in this ship of fools. And yet it was I who saw her as unhappy, cut off, an outcast. Perhaps I was only projecting. Certainly she was full of bustle and busyness, making her little nests, defecating in her special enamel pot with cover, never smearing or swearing like the others. Her name was Hazel and she had been in that room for thirteen years. NO KNOWN RELATIVES. I saw it on her card. When she died she would probably be cremated, not even given the dubious honour of a crêpe-paper nightie and a pauper's grave. Who had discovered her affliction, her terrible power to hurt? Mrs. Reynolds shrugged. "I have no idea. She was transferred here, years ago, from another hospital." Why did she smile at me? Why did she not cry out and curse as Cain had done, as I had done, "My punishment is more than I can bear!"

Next to Hazel were the two empty rooms and then, closest to the nurses' station, was Beatrice. I still don't know what was technically wrong with her. She was certainly retarded and probably schizophrenic as well. I was not allowed to look at the files — Mrs. Kolodzy and Mrs. Reynolds had very strong feelings about the privacy of their patients' histories. "Not that we don't trust you, love, it's just that they have so little." Beatrice could have been seventeen or thirty — a great long creature with coarse skin and twisted limbs. She had coarse reddish hair on her arms, her legs, her face. Spoke from the back of her throat in thick gutturals, like a caveman. With her broken teeth, her nostrils close together like a monkey's, her excessive hairiness and her strange way of speaking she was like something emerging into, but not quite, man. Or maybe the reverse — a girl in the process of turning into a monster. She was the only one on 88 who wore proper pajamas — or pajama tops at least (for Judith never wore anything that *her* relatives brought) — little nylon, lace-trimmed jackets and baby dolls which looked terribly grotesque on her big, angular, tortured body. The pores of her face were large and clogged with blackheads, and the nurses tied ribbons on her greasy, reddish hair. The first time I saw her I ran away and wept in the staff room. Florence Reynolds came after me.

"Are you crying for her or for yourself?"

"I don't know, I don't know, I don't know."

"Is it because she's young?" I nodded. But was that really it?

"Don't forget, my love, they were all young once. Babies, little kids playing hopscotch or Mother May I."

"But they weren't all mad so young."

"True. They weren't all mad so young or born so goddamned

ugly and helpless as this one." She lit a cigarette. "I want you to go back and get used to her."

"I can't. She repulses me."

"You didn't even think you could work on this ward, remember?"

"I remember."

"All right. Get going then."

But I never got used to that girl. I was afraid my disgust and terror would show in my face and it probably did, for occasionally, as I sat by her bed going through the boxes of old greeting cards which she loved, picking out the ones with glitter on them or a ribbon or a raised bit of cheap satin that said "Mother" in fancy script, she would suddenly turn on me and grab my hair, pulling harder and harder until I yelled and one of the nurses had to come and pry her loose. Then they would scold her and she would cry with great raw primordial sobs — horrible for me to listen to — sitting propped up in her baby-doll nightie. Or work herself into a completely inarticulate rage, shouting, grunting, struggling with the nurse until she had to be restrained and taken away to the baths. The cards lay scattered on the floor.

> Although you're miles away today
> And we are far apart
> The love which flows from me to you
> Unites our absent hearts
> For Mother dear
> You've always been
> My angel and my guide
> So let this little verse express
> What's hidden deep inside.

The room was full of the smell of Beatrice's rage, and as I bent over to tidy up my face was hot with shame. ("I'm sorry sorry sorry.") The old ladies did not really touch me, chiefly, I suspect, because of their great age. But Beatrice, who *could have been seventeen!* Crippled in mind, in body, her anger toward me, who not only could pick up her greeting cards with such ease and walk in and out of her room as I pleased but who refused her love because I couldn't stand to *look* at her, seemed entirely justified. I wondered who was really the monster, the crippled girl or I. Mrs. Kolodzy and Mrs. Reynolds, whom I had thought, at first, were simply tough, cynical, *hardened* women, had great compassion for this girl. The bits of ribbon in her hair, the cards solicited from the wastebaskets of other wards, the firm but reassuring hugs when she was hallucinating — all these were genuine personal, not professional, responses to a maimed and bleeding soul.

Beatrice had an auntie who came to see her every other week and brought the baby-doll pajamas, the comic books, the dime-store necklaces and penny candy. She was a grey-faced middle-aged woman in a shiny black dress of the kind my grade school teachers had always seemed to favour. She lived in Cortland and came in on the bus. Sat by Beatrice's bedside and held her twisted hands. Mrs. Reynolds told me the aunt worked as a cleaning lady and had never failed to turn up on the ward every second Wednesday. An old woman with broken shoes and broken English who often wore men's carpet slippers on her swollen feet and kissed the mad girl, stroked her forehead, spoke to her in a low, reassuring croon.

"So," she said to me one day. "You are the new girl." I nodded, afraid to look her in the eye.

"Be goot to my poor shild — is Gott who vill bless you." Patted my hand as she had patted Beatrice's. Went slowly and heavily down the corridor carrying her empty shopping bag.

I think hers was the first utterly unselfish love I had ever seen in my life and I was deeply affected by it. The woman was old. What if some Wednesday she did not show up? Died in her sleep? Was knocked down by a car? What would happen then?

On my days off, lying in the backyard on a blanket, letting the sun burn away the sickness and stench which I felt must cling to me, I tried to imagine Beatrice seeing me. No one had ever wanted to be me before. I had always wanted to be somebody, *anybody* else.

MISSING HEIRESS FOUND
CHOOSES TO RETURN
TO HOMELAND

Dear Robert Walker
I am 11 years old and
very unhappy

I felt the sunlight licking at my straight legs. Clenched and unclenched my hands. Shut my eyes and tried to become gross, deformed, inarticulate. The helpless tears ran down my face and I covered my shame with a magazine, as though I'd had too much sun. It was no use no use no use. I could not imagine. Could not bear.... My mother was right: I was cold. Like the Snow Queen of the fairy tale, other people did not concern me. My grounds for rejecting Beatrice were monstrous because they were strictly aesthetic. If Beatrice had been my mother? My sister? My *child*?

The next morning I asked my father for some roses. It was a beautiful day. Someone had been up very early on our street, cutting the grass. The sweet smell of it was everywhere.

"Sure. What d'you want 'em for?"

"Oh. Just to brighten up the ward." He gave me pretty well everything that was left.

"Are you sure?"

"Yeah. They've passed their prime anyway."

I rolled the stems in a wet washcloth and then made a wrapper of wax paper. I had never really liked my father's roses. The colours were the pinks and yellows of ladies' underwear; they were overblown and voluptuous and their scent was very sweet. Still, they were an offering, and I knew he might not part with his precious "glads" and dahlias which were just coming into bloom.

As I waited for the elevator two of the men from 89 looked at my flowers and smiled.

"Are those for us, Princess?"

"Give us a sniff." The tall one stuck his nose into the roses, "accidentally" pushing against my breasts.

"Oh. Sorry. Got carried away with the fragrance." I tried not to cry.

The night nurse and the PN said, "What lovely flowers! Where are you going to put them?"

I was arranging them in a big jar when Mrs. Reynolds walked in.

"What beautiful flowers."

"They're for Beatrice," I said defensively. She gave me a strange look, then nodded and plugged the kettle in.

"I'll be right back," I said.

Beatrice's door was open and she lay with her eyes closed. The sheet and coverlet were stained with her breakfast. There were bits of egg clinging to the hairs by her mouth. Even with the window open the room smelled foul.

"Beatty," I said, "I brought you some flowers." The windowsill was too narrow, so I drew up the chair and put the flowers on it, next to her bed. Then stood there, uncertain.

"Beatty, there's some flowers for you. From my father's garden. We picked for you just now." Still with her eyes closed, but I knew she was awake. I took the roses off the chair, sat down in it and held the jar of flowers on my lap.

"I brought these," I said. "For you." In the dull pale brown and cream of the room my father's roses glowed with a warmth and colour I had never seen in them on the outside. Perhaps out there they were bleached out by the intense blue sky, the grass, the brassy marigolds.

She opened her eyes and struggled to sit up. I didn't help her, just sat there holding out the flowers.

"Let me give you one to hold." I picked out a white one with a creamy-pink tinge. Broke off all the thorns and put it in her hands.

"Nigh-seh," she said. "Nigh-seh."

"Smell it." Her head fell forward into the petals. Then she sat up again and trembling, wrenched off some of the petals and put them in her mouth. Chewed them. Swallowed them. Picked off some more.

"Here," said Mrs. Kolodzy from the doorway, "you'll spoil

your lunch." She took the jar of flowers from me, and Mrs. Reynolds brought in the typewriter table from the nurses' station.

"There," she said, "now you can look at them all day."

Pollen clung to Beatrice's face, mixing with the yellow bits of egg. She shook her head and began to weep, rocking back and forth, a horrible creaking sound coming from her throat.

"What's the matter with her?" I cried, desperate. "What does she want?"

"I don't know, love. Perhaps she'd rather eat them than look at them."

The mad girl's cries filled the little room, bounced off the walls, the ceiling, my heart.

"Would they hurt her?"

"I guess not. If your dad doesn't use any spray on them."

"He doesn't. He's terrified of things like that."

"O.K. Let's give them to her. But not all at once."

By the end of the week she had eaten every one of them.

I wept into my pillow o sorry sorry sorry.

"What the hell d'you suppose she wants to *eat* them for?" said Mrs. Reynolds, exasperated for once.

"God knows."

"Just be sure you don't get carried away and bring her lilies of the valley," said Mrs. Kolodzy, who was very keen on gardening. "They're poison. We'd never explain that to the boys in Albany."

"Who wants to go at eleven-thirty?"

"I do, Isobel can go with me."

("Hey, Florence," called the young men from 89 and 91, "lend us the princess for a quick fuck." "Got some flowers for us, darling?" they called. "A little kiss?" "Some token of your affection?")

sixteen

When I walked up the aisle past Eleanor La Duce, she would point her finger at me and shout, "You're a hoor! You're nothing but a filthy hoor!"

"I think it's your skirts, love," said Mrs. Reynolds. "It's that one with the roosters that particularly upsets her."

But I wondered sometimes if Eleanor, like the silent, rigid woman in the third side ward, didn't see something in me that I had, so far, successfully managed to hide. At seventeen I was still a virgin but felt that great heaviness of desire in my legs and stomach whenever I was with a man I thought attractive. (Or sometimes just whenever I was with a man.) The summer after Christopher had died I went back to the Saturday night square dances for a while and fooled around with some of the boys from the camp; but it was all too painful, and as Jane was not there much that last summer I had no real impetus to keep on going. My favourite recreation became, instead, taking the biggest boat out and roaring, restless, up and down the lake, sometimes stopping at the little island to lie on the sand in my new two-piece Jantzen and try to recapture the sensation of Chris's leg stretched out against my own. I had no boyfriends in town to think about. Boys talked to me in class sometimes but nobody except those I labelled "creeps" (i.e., unknown or unattractive) ever called me up or walked me home. My mother worried terribly about this, bought me clothes and gave me perms, even let me have a boy-girl party which was a complete disaster. Somebody fused the lights with a penny and a girl I thought was much more unattractive than I was sat on the lap of the handsomest boy in the class and picked out "Heart and Soul" over and over again on my grandmother's out-of-tune piano. Several of the boys I had invited stayed away, and girls sat in corners and chatted about sorority (to which I did not belong) or said they were sorry but they had to get home early, they had promised to help their mother in the morning.

My mother bawled me out about the smoking and necking, the noise, the crack in the glass-topped dining room table. I knew that I had let these kids "walk all over me," as she said (or screamed, standing in the door of my bedroom, her old bathrobe held together by a safety pin), and that "nobody respects a girl who plays fast and loose." "If that's the way your fancy friends behave, then you're better off without them."

Jane had escaped from all this only by accepting second best, joining KΨ when she was turned down by ΦK and θΣ, going to movies with Jewish boys (she even brought one to church on Christmas Eve. My mother walked out, weeping, and sat in the freezing car until the service was over), becoming "big" in Miss Foley's public speaking class, the Drama Club. She adopted a noisy, rather bold manner but worked very hard at school and usually got A's. I envied her her courage and her phone calls but wanted "the best" or nothing. My mother encouraged me. If I was not pledged to one of the big sororities it was not my fault but the fault of our circumstances. If the captain of the basketball team never looked my way it was because I didn't live on Riverside Drive or because I was a "nice girl." I had no desire to be a nice girl but still found myself obeying the rigid social rules which governed just what a girl could do — any girl — to attract the boys. Kids walked by in the corridors, hand in hand. Girls were "pinned" to boys, wore gardenia corsages to the proms. I invited the handsomest boy in class to the ΦK winter formal — girls could ask boys to this and "anyone" could go — months ahead of time; miraculously he said a reluctant yes. (I did not know my mother had phoned his mother the night before.) I tried on formal after formal in the Junior Deb Shop at Wiggins, Pollard and Baines, the Sweet Sixteen at MacLeod's, Young Misses at David's, Young World at Joseph's. I remember the dress we finally chose. I thought it was absolutely beautiful. Layers of cocoa-coloured net over a taffeta slip and underbodice (strapless, of course, as was then the style — I planned to stuff the top with old stockings, as I felt my breasts were much too small. "Rat-Bites," my sister called them once). Two beautiful rosettes of real ostrich plume in pale, pale, creamy-brown. We found suede shoes with very high heels in exactly the same colour. I hoped he would call up and ask the colour of my dress, as "they" were supposed to do.

My mother was very excited about the formal. Bought us each a long cape — mine in emerald velvet, Jane's in creamy-white wool (she was wearing black — very daring). I went to André's and had my hair set; so did Jane. I soaked in the bath and splashed myself with Elizabeth Arden's "Blue Grass" — my favourite scent. (Jane was wearing "Tigress" — I heard her giggling to her boyfriend on the phone.) When my father grumbled about the new clothes my mother took him aside, in the dining room, and told him that this was "a big chance" and "the least he could do."

Before supper the corsages arrived from Munshaw's. Two plain white boxes tied up in thin green ribbon. I didn't want to open mine; I just wanted to sit and hold the box, to *imagine* the contents. Jane opened hers. Inside the green paper was a wrist corsage of tiny red roses. My mother, who didn't entirely approve of her boyfriend, thoroughly approved of his choice of flowers.

"So why shouldn't it be good? I told him exactly what to get," Jane said, adopting a Jewish accent, and my mother winced.

"Open yours, Isobel."

"Yes. Open it, honey. And then we'll put it in the fridge. Supper's ready."

"Later."

"Isobel, don't be so silly." Even my father put down his paper and urged me to find out what was inside the box. I undid it slowly, not wanting to share the moment with these people. Something yellow lay hidden underneath the almost opaque green paper. I folded the edges back.

"Oh."

"Lovely."

"That sure is a swell corsage." Carnations the colour of clotted cream, spicy, exciting. He had never asked the colour of my dress, had hardly spoken to me, except in French class, where he sat behind me and copied all my answers since the night I phoned him up and asked him to the dance. There was a small white card enclosed, "Jorgen." It was not his handwriting but never mind. Maybe his mother had helped him choose. I could see them discussing it together — he was describing me. "Small, you know. Slim. With auburn hair and big blue eyes."

"Well, then, she *must* have carnations. Creamy ones. To bring out her skin tones. I know just the thing!"

Perhaps he loved me. It was not completely impossible. I put the lid back on the box and we went in to supper — nothing oniony that would make our breath smell; nothing that might "repeat." Soup and cream cheese on Boston brown bread. Jane sat with her bathrobe slightly undone, her black "Merry Widow" showing, her legs crossed high. Her nails were an incredible scarlet, as though she might leave bloodstains on the tablecloth. I was both a little afraid and a little ashamed of her. I felt she was slightly vulgar, slightly overdone, not realizing then that this was her way of defying those who had rejected us. After all, we had only bought tickets to the ΦK formal; we weren't among the chosen few who *sold* them.

Mother started talking about a dance she went to when she lived in New York City. A tea dance in a big hotel. She wore moss green crêpe de chine and little golden slippers. I couldn't

166

imagine it but smiled at her anyway, peeping over the great benevolent bath of my own happiness.

The telephone rang. Jane rose from her languid position with incredible speed.

"That's probably Nathan — to see if the flowers came. I'll get it."

My mother winced again at the sound of this name and then began to give me a friendly lecture on what to do if there was drink around or being offered under the table. Jane came back in, quickly.

"It's for you, fece-face."

"Jane!" But she didn't bother me. He had called to ask if I liked the flowers. He just wanted to talk to me. He wanted to ask if he'd mentioned the party at Heather's house after the dance.

"Listen," he said, and I could tell from his voice that it was none of these things. "I can't go."

"You can't go," I repeated dully.

"No. My grandmother just died a few minutes ago. My parents think it wouldn't be right."

"No. No. I guess it wouldn't be right."

"Well ... I'm sorry." (But I didn't think he was.)

"Thank you for the flowers."

"Yeah.... Well ... see you in school."

I put down the phone and went upstairs to take the stuffing out of my bra. To take off my expensive, expensive, heelless, toeless Hanes stockings before they got a run. To put my lovely brown dress away in its big striped box. To lie on my bed and wonder why I never learned.

My mother said it was an outrage and she had a good mind to call up Mrs. Johannsen.... And I said if she did that I would walk out of the house and never come back again. My father, of course, hovered in the doorway and said it was a goddamned shame. Jane suggested I go anyway, with her and Nathan and their friends.

I wore the beautiful corsage to church the next day. Jorgen wasn't there, but the minister did mention his grandmother who had been "called away suddenly" and for whom we were asked to pray. I felt a little better. There *was* a grandmother; there *had been* a death. But I still couldn't believe that he would have stayed home if I had been one of the other, prettier, girls or even a real sorority girl. On the Monday we avoided each other's eyes as we walked into class. The party at Heather's had been a scream.

So the summer after Christopher died I roared around in the old boat looking for someone, anyone to prove me attractive again. The sunsets, the beige sand, the cool nights and heat-filled hazy days: all were the same. Only I was changed: had loved, lost, suffered. I read a lot of poetry, lying on the sand or in an old striped hammock stretched between two pine trees. Wondered if my time with Chris was the only sip from the cup of joy which I was to be allowed. And then I discovered Digger Tremaine, the anthropoid lifeguard at the public campsite: hairy college boy from Hamilton. Broken-toothed and with a face like a wise gorilla. He sat all day in bathing trunks and gob hat, high up in his lifeguard's chair. I ran my boat up on the beach one day to have a look at the campsite and he shouted for me to get out of the swimming area. Embarrassed, I flooded the engine and he climbed down to give me a good lecture.

I had never seen anyone so hairy. He had hair on the backs of his fingers, hair in his ears, hair in a long swath from his breast-bone to underneath his trunks somewhere. It was very hard for me to look at him without blushing.

"You know better than to bring a boat in here."

Red-faced, I pulled hard on the starting rope. "I ... won't ... do ... it ... a-gain ..." (through clenched teeth).

"And you'll shear a pin running a boat up on a beach like that." (As if I didn't know.)

"Why ... don't ... you ... go ... save ... lives ... or ... something?"

"Why don't you wait a few minutes and *then* try and start the engine?" (I could hear him thinking, "Stupid bitch.")

I sat on the beach with my back to the campsite. The little island was straight ahead of me, and way, way, way over to the left was Harry's aluminum-painted boathouse, winking in the sun. Behind me city people with a week or two week's vacation set up tents, shook out sleeping bags, made lunch or called to truant dogs and children. The lifeguard sat down beside me.

"I've seen you before."

I shrugged.

"At the Saturday-night dance. You don't come any more."

I shrugged again and let the sand fall through my fingers.

"Cat got your tongue?"

("Shut up," said somebody's mother, from inside one of the tents, "or I'll really give you something to cry about.") When I figured that five minutes had gone by, I got up, dusted myself off and willed the motor to start. It did, and I accepted the lifeguard's push with a little nod but still refused to speak.

"Come again," he said, laughing at me. "I don't bite."

I thought about him that night. Bandy-legged and with a gravelly voice. Short. Dark. Possibly Jewish. At any rate a boy who would never be accepted at the country club (except as a lifeguard perhaps). But sexy. My God yes. I lay in bed thinking about what it would be like to "go all the way" with a guy like that lifeguard. No doubt he'd been around. I didn't want any fumbling, inept, excuse-making boy to initiate me into the mysteries of sex. If I couldn't have love I would settle for expertise. I wished I had big floppy breasts — I felt that would appeal to a man like him. It was no good stuffing your swimsuit if you were planning to let it be torn off at the crucial moment. I decided to let him seduce me.

I went back to the campsite the next day and the next. Told him I'd come to apologize for my rude behaviour. He looked at me and I knew he knew what I was really after. We talked. He was not as stupid as he looked. And very gentle with the little kids, who shrieked and squealed and flailed their pale arms in the shallow water.

"Digger! Look at me, Digger. I'm swimmin'!" "Digger, look at me!"

I lay on my belly, on my back. Below the tall lifeguard's chair. Pretending I was Digger's girl. The pressure of the sun against my back, my belly, was terrible, terrible, terrible. He didn't ask me to go to the dance on Saturday night — I stayed home and sulked, not even able to weep away my tension because of the thin curtain which separated me from my mother and father. The vibration of the bass fiddle went into my legs and twanged against the very centre of my being. I stuffed the pillow in my mouth.

The next week I became even more daring.

"D'you ever go up to T-Lake Falls?" I said in what I hoped was a casual yet seductive manner. "It's very pretty up there." Lying on my elbow like the girls in the suntan-lotion ads. Letting some sand drift through my fingers. He was rolling himself a cigarette and looked even more peculiar than usual, for he had burned his nose badly and had it covered in a thick white layer of barrier cream. He lit the "smoke" and spat a couple of pieces of tobacco through his teeth.

"Who says?"

"I say. We've been hiking up to the Falls since I was a little girl."

"And now you're a big girl." He grinned at me and I blushed.

"I wasn't inviting you to come with me. I was just asking if you'd ever been there."

"Oh, I see." Scratching at all that matted hair on his chest. "Well, no. I haven't been up T-Lake Falls."

"You should go sometime." Turned over on my stomach — pretending sleep.

My mother said, "I don't know if you should stay out so long on the lake, dear. I begin to worry." She and Aunt Hettie were stringing beans on the front porch. They looked so old so old so old — so unloved and undesired. I couldn't bear to turn out like that.

"I only go over to the island. It's very peaceful there. When Jane comes up there'll be more to do."

"Plenty to do right here in this house, honey, if you look around." Aunt Hettie gave the porch glider a smug little push with her foot.

That wasn't worth answering, so I went inside and flopped down on the big double bed. Tiny points of sunlight came through the old cracked green window shade. I was burning, burning, burning. I couldn't get my mind away from my body. No man had ever wanted me — not even Christopher now that I thought about it. Why not? Why didn't he even try? Was I really unattractive? (Secretly I thought of myself as quite good-looking although I know my mother's attempts to make me "pretty" indicated that I certainly wasn't *that*.) Why should the men have so much power? Look at Digger. He was really gross. Yet all the girls at the campsite flirted with him, brought him pop or cold beer, asked him to tie up their straps. "Real tight now. I don't want this thing falling off in the water." Giggling if he gave them a slap on the behind. Just because he was a life-guard and played fullback for his college. Just because he was a man. I vowed I wouldn't go back. Sat on the porch that night with my grandfather, my father, my mother, my aunt; male and female but all sexless, somehow (except maybe Harry; he still had something very male and exciting about him — a fleck of gold still shining in the rock his life now was). We watched the great bleeding sunset and then the Northern Lights, very faint and far away.

> My bonny lies over the ocean
> My bonny lies over the sea
> My father lay over my mother
> and that's how they got little me.

If one thought about *that* it was quite incredible.

In his room Harry had a small drawing which showed the evolution of the engagement ring.

Engagement Ring
Wedding Ring
Teething Ring

The last was a baby's face, screaming. Sex led to babies, but not if you were careful. I'd seen lots of French Letters in the parks, in gutters. Boys carried them in their billfolds. If a girl did get "caught" she went out West for her "asthma" before the baby began to show. But you were supposed to wait, if you were a "nice girl." What the hell for? The whole ethic of love, marriage and then sex seemed crazy to me. I went out and walked barefoot down the path to the beach.

"Isobel, where are you going?"

"Just for a walk."

I could predict my mother's words as soon as she thought I was out of earshot: "I don't know what to do about Isobel, she's such a difficult child." Counting over the sacrifices she'd made, the "doing without," the "insults and humiliations."

Aunt Hettie sat with her hands folded across her lap, having a little bedtime conversation with the Lord, smiling. "Now I ask you, Lord, if that isn't what happens to those poor folks who turn their back on You!"

My father, lighting another cigarette, would worry about me in a vague, wistful way. But too overwhelmed by his own position. Wondering if he should buy some gas for the boat, whether he's even got enough spare change for smokes for the rest of the summer. Worried about having to drive that old car down to Utica and back to pick up Jane on the first. What if a tire? Feeling hungry — wishing he dared go and see if there was any leftover chicken in the fridge.

Harry, silent in his special chair by the side of the porch. Gazing unseeing at what? Life? Death? His amused, slightly contemptuous smile on his face. Did he care what happened, was happening to me? Did he really understand? What prevented me from going to him and telling. "Oh, Harry, I'm so alone, so alone, so alone." Our old cocker spaniel padded ahead of me down the dark path. She had been spayed as soon as she was old enough. Was as sexless as the four who sat above me on the porch. No exciting terriers or Springer spaniels sniffed at her!

I stayed away from Digger for three days. Helped Harry make a bird feeding station, picked huge pailfuls of blueberries for Aunt Hettie, let my mother ramble on to me about her past. Agreed with her that life wasn't always easy, that we didn't always get what we wanted right away, that nice girls had a harder time of it than most. Went down to Red's Baits with my father and willed myself not to feel impatient while he gassed about the weather and the coming election, the best way to fry brook trout. The bait house was dark and cool and sensuous and smelled of rich damp earth. We came away with little white delicatessen cartons full of dobson and nightwalkers. Passing the campsite on the way home.

"Would you like to stay at a place like that?" I asked him.

"Jesus. No. All them kids and dogs jammed up right next to one another." But I wondered if he wouldn't have liked the idea of men sitting around campfires swapping fish stories — things like that. I knew Digger was down below the campgrounds on the beach, maybe sitting up in his chair and looking for my old green motorboat?

"Goin' up to fish the stream by T-Lake Mountain," my father said. "Tomorrow early. Want to come?" We hadn't been fishing together for about five years and I was surprised.

"Oh. No. I don't think so."

"Suit yourself." I felt ashamed, for I knew he would be pleased; but in my present mood I'd be too restless, too irritable, would scare the fish away.

There was a note for me in the mailbox. No postage stamp, so he must have been out in the camp truck.

"Come up T-Falls with me tomorrow. Bring your boat over to the campsite and say you'll be out all morning." No signature. I quickly shoved it down the front of my shirt.

"Goddamn bills," my father was muttering, sorting the rest of the mail. He hadn't even noticed.

The next morning I was awake before my father. Heard him heavy-footed, searching out his clothes, padding to the bathroom, making sandwiches and coffee. My mother was always irritated with him for not fixing a lunch the night before.

"And eat goddamned soggy bread?"

"It's better than waking up the whole house with your clatter." (I heard Mother get up to shush him — heard him retreat down the back steps, start the car, manoeuvre it around and head down the road. Why had he picked today? Why had Digger? If I didn't show up at the campsite Digger probably wouldn't ask me again. The nearest public telephone was at

Trinity Lake — I could hardly risk telephoning from the cottage. I would just have to go over there and tell him why it was off, impossible. (But had taken a bath the night before, washed my hair and done it up in pin curls. Was right now up and packing sandwiches myself — big he-man sandwiches of tuna fish salad. Aunt Hettie's buttermilk cookies.)

"Is it all right, Aunt Hettie, if I take this chicken leg? I won't be back for dinner." I had done all the breakfast dishes, hung the dish towels out on the revolving clothesline, laid the table for dinner (a practice Aunt Hettie liked but which I found rather vulgar). Told my mother I was going over to the island for most of the day. Was taking my French books with me.

"Just don't get too much sun." It was all so easy and yet I was so obvious, I think now, that I'm very surprised my mother and my aunt, both extremely suspicious by nature, didn't catch on to me.

Two oranges. Two paper napkins. I put my bathing suit on underneath my jeans. A wet washcloth in a bread wrapper. In case I ... But no. I was going over to tell him it was crazy, too risky, impossible. A thermos full of lemonade. My sneakers tied around my neck.

"I'll see you later." (Stop me Stop me Stop me.) Down the forest path, still cool from the night before. Unlock the boathouse. Get out the oars, the life-preserver cushion. Untie the boat. I watched myself doing all these things as though I were doing them for the last time. The lake and sky were a clear Madonna blue as I set out. It was such a beautiful morning that I would have rowed if I hadn't thought I might get myself too sweaty. It seemed a shame to break the silence with a motorboat. I kept the throttle nearly all the way in, set off at as slow a speed as possible. The old dog yelped disconsolately from the shore. (Back. Back. Back. Back. Back.) I thought about crazy things: how he was going to react when I told him we couldn't go. At what point the man put his sheath on. Or did I? Would I bleed? Were there things I was supposed to do to him and didn't know about?

Past the island, deserted, the little beach just beginning to warm up. The water here was very deep and clear. I could see the sharp rocks down below. Past two old men in straw hats, one at each end of their boat, trolling for lake trout. Around past little unknown cottages. Painted boats tied up and perfectly motionless. It was a still moment. Time cut out and preserved like a paperweight under the bright blue dome of the sky. The two old men were now just tiny figures to bring the eye back in a landscape painting. A still moment before God. Only Isobel was moving, now under the shadow of Panther Mountain. It was suddenly cold and I shivered.

Digger helped me pull the boat away up on the sand. He paid some early-morning kid a quarter to see that nobody messed about with it.

"Sure, Digger. Just let anybody try and touch it." Eight or nine years old with a horrible scab on one knee and a Brooklyn Dodgers sweatshirt.

Digger had on his jeans and tee shirt. Hair sprouted from the sleeves and neck. Suddenly my stomach turned over.

"Listen, Digger, I ..."

"You what?" He was looking for the car keys among a great assortment of keys he'd taken out of his pocket.

"Nothing. Forget it." He stopped walking, rocked back and forth on the balls of his feet, grinned.

"I thought you were the girl who wanted to climb T-Lake Mountain."

"I did. I do. Let's go." (Stop me, O lady frying sausages over a campfire. Stop me, Brooklyn Dodger kid. Stop me, lake, sky, trees. I can't go through with this.)

We sat up high in the cab of the pick-up truck, the landscape a blur as we sped past. Digger and his girl at 9:30 on a summer morning. We parked in the meadow below the beginning of the path. There were two cars already there. One of them was my father's.

"Digger."

"Yeah?" Screwing some wax out of his ear with his little finger.

"That's my father's car."

"What's he doing here?"

"Fishing the trout stream. That's what I was trying to tell you."

"Oh shit," he said. "Oh shit." I was relieved, saved, apologetic. "I'm sorry."

He sat a minute thick hands still holding the steering wheel. Then shook his head.

"It doesn't matter."

"Doesn't matter!"

"Nope. I'll go first and locate him. Then you can sneak past that bit. It'll be okay."

I couldn't really imagine what my father would do if he saw Digger and me — or even just me. I could tell him I decided to climb the mountain, but how did I get there then? I set off in a boat. You could only get to T-Lake Mountain by road. I was truly scared now. Not really of my father but of what my father would say. Of what he would tell my mother.

"It's too risky. He'll see us."

"Not unless you want him to."

"Oh, I don't, really I don't." I described my father: a short, plump man in rubber waders and an old felt hat. He would be wearing an old khaki-coloured shirt and a small red Community Chest feather in his hat.

"Got it. Let's hope the other guy is tall and thin and wearing a bandanna."

We climbed down and I counted to two hundred before I followed him. He had the sandwiches and thermos in a small backpack, a blanket rolled above it.

The climb up T-Lake Mountain is nothing, really. The elevation is only a little over three thousand feet. The path is very narrow but easy to follow. To your left as you go up you can hear the distant murmur of the trout stream through the trees. At points the path goes along the stream and one is always a little surprised to come upon a solitary fisherman, waist deep in the cold, delicious-looking water, or sitting on a flat rock having a quiet smoke. I had fished these waters with my father — I had climbed to the Falls and to the fire tower beyond with Mother and Daddy and Jane. At one point the trail crosses over a tiny log bridge and you suddenly find yourself on the other side of the stream, listening to its whisperings with your right ear rather than your left.

It was strange to walk all this alone, knowing Digger was ahead of me, my father somewhere up above. I took off my shoes and walked barefoot, silently, past rocks blanketed in pale-green moss, past trees that had been there for a century at least. Twisted, gnarled. Like old people with arthritic joints.

I walked for nearly an hour before I saw Digger, his finger to his lips, coming back down the path toward me.

"It's a bitch," he said. "He's right at a place where he'd have to be dead or blind drunk not to see you if you pass." I stood passive, the backs of my legs aching just a little, waiting for him to decide.

"We'll skirt around through the forest."

"Won't he wonder what it is?"

"Naw. He'll just assume it's deer."

Which is what we did — making a wide arc around the stream, me stumbling behind Digger, catching my feet on vines and bits of root. Coming back out again farther up.

"D'you want to go all the way to the Falls?"

"I don't care."

"Let's stop soon. I'll find us a good place."

Did my heart thump from the exertion (it was steeper now) or the fear? If I called out, what would my father do? Would he recognize my voice and if so respond to it? "Daddy Daddy Daddy." Digger went ahead again to reconnoitre.

"C'mon. There's a meadow just across the stream." His feet were bare and his rolled-up jeans were wet along the edges. He took my hand and we crossed together. The water was terribly cold and the smooth brown rocks were slippery.

"Careful." His strong hand covering my own.

We ate in a meadow full of black-eyed Susans. I had forgotten the salt.

"Doesn't matter. S'great." Gnawing at the chicken leg (the way he would gnaw at me?). We peeled oranges and let the juice run down our faces. He wiped his hands on his jeans and said, rather absently, "Take off your clothes."

I stood up, ashamed of my thin, small-breasted body. Ashamed of the heaviness in my legs. Removed my shirt and jeans and stood there in my two-piece bathing suit. Digger came and put his hands on my shoulders. (He was only a few inches taller than I was.)

"*All* of them. Shall I help you?"

I nodded dumbly. I could see the hair in his nostrils, smell his orange-scented breath. He undid the clasp of my bathing suit top and pulled it off me. I tried to put my arms across my chest.

"Don't," he said. Gently. "Don't be silly." He examined my breasts with his eyes and hands. I hadn't realized that they ... I never ...

"You've got good nipples," he said. "Good for nursing." It wasn't me, it was some stranger who stood there and let this creature suck at me. Who unzipped his pants to discover the great bruised-looking thing she had never actually seen before. And so much hair! Were they all or was it only?

"Digger. Digger."

But he moaned and turned away, still clasping my hand to him.

"No."

"Why not? Why not?" I was ready to be initiated into anything and everything. I was just a burning bush in the middle of a summer meadow.

He sat up, dropped my hand and pulled on his pants.

"Isobel, do you really want your first fuck to be a guy who has a football scholarship to a second-rate university? Who doesn't love you or you him and who may want you like hell but only temporarily and maybe only once?"

"Yes. Yes Yes Yes Yes."

"Well, I don't. You've just got the hots for me because you're bored and lonely. I'm not the guy you really want."

"You can't say that. How do you know?"

"I know because I know. I'm twenty-two and you're sixteen — that's one of the reasons I know. You don't even like me most of the time. If I wasn't the lifeguard and the whole thing wasn't a great big adventure, you'd pass me by on the street."

"I wouldn't. I wouldn't." Crying now, but knew what he spoke was the truth.

He lay down beside me and began to stroke me very gently. It was the most exquisite feeling I had ever had. Very gently. Talking to me all the time.

"Listen. You're a good kid. You've got a lovely body. A bit scrawny maybe but give it time." He parted my legs and continued stroking me.

"You've got lovely skin. So soft. Lovely. D'you like that?"

"Yes. Oh, yes."

"This is all you really need. Don't get involved with just anyone because you're hot. That's a stupid way to behave and you're not stupid. D'you like that as well?"

"Yes yes yes. Yes yes."

He stroked me harder all the time, but never hurt me. Talked to me, lectured me, all the time bringing me up and up to a point of such incredible excitement that I couldn't lie still. His hand was wet with my desire.

"I'm doing this because you need to get rid of all this emotion, d'you understand? And because I like you. You're a weird sort of kid but you're okay. And you've got a lovely body, don't forget it. Lovely, lovely, lovely." Then he bent down and began to lick me. I was shocked and excited beyond belief. Nowhere had I read dreamed imagined oh oh oh. And it was as though a great bell had clanged down there and was vibrating inside the whole of me.

He sat up and smoothed my hair.

"You're really going to be somethin' when you grow up."

I kept my eyes closed. Against the sun. Against Digger. Against my new world. All my energy had flowed out into his mouth and I don't think I could have moved if I'd wanted to. It had been so beautiful, so beautiful. But incredibly lonely out there beyond the meadow. Beyond mind. Beyond control.

There was a terrible bulge in the crotch of his jeans. I tried not to look.

"It's all right," he said. "I'll talk it down."

We gathered up our things and went back down the mountain. I didn't know whether I felt betrayed or grateful. Both, I guess. When he shoved me off at the campsite he said, "Come back and see me sometime." So I knew that we were finished. That the day had been an end, not beginning.

And I still didn't know what it *really* felt like to make love with a man. Was still searching, seeking, hoping.

"Sorry," said one of the jokers on 89, bumping into me as we waited for the elevator.

"You're a hoor!" screamed Eleanor La Duce. "You're nothing but a filthy hoor!"

I waited for the summer to bring me my deliverance.

Harry came to me in a dream. He had death spots on the back of his hands. When he turned around he had no back, just a piece of cardboard which had propped him up. "Isobel," said Harry's voice, speaking out from the back of the cardboard, "Isobel, where are you?" I didn't answer, but lit a cigarette instead and leaned against the lamppost. Casually I dropped the match near Harry's cardboard feet. He went up beautifully and without complaint. Mind you, I couldn't see his face, of course.

seventeen

At the beginning of my fourth week, the director stepped out of his principal's office and touched me on the arm as I was waiting for the elevator.

"Isobel, can I see you for a minute?"

I followed him down the hall.

"What's an old geezer like him got," said one of the jokers on 99, "that you and I ain't got?" My ears burned. They said it loudly so Mike would be sure to hear.

"Do those characters bother you?"

"Sometimes."

"Don't pay any attention."

"I don't," I said, lying.

"Good. Good." He began fiddling with the papers on his desk.

"We've got another assignment for you."

"I looked at him, unbelieving.

"Another assignment?"

"Yeah. To the OR. We'd like you to start this morning. The girls up there have been having terrible trouble with the orderly — we had to let him go."

"But what about 88?"

"What about it?" He peered at me through his thick glasses.

"I mean, I'm settled there. I know the routine. I get on well with the nurses." I was very cold.

("Turn away, Isobel," said my mother, referring to a dead dog in the street. "Don't look.")

"I know you do, I know you do." Impaling a truant memorandum on his spindle. "As a matter of fact, Florence's been chewing me out already for taking you away from them."

"Why then?"

"Because there's nobody else we can spare right now. If we find somebody you can go back to 88. You're quick and you're eager to learn." He came around the desk and gave me a little pat, the way he had done on that first morning, and took down a new set of keys.

"Can I keep the ones for eighty-eight?"

"Well, you really should turn them in. However ..." He walked me to the elevator himself.

"I've been meaning to tell you how pleased we are with the way you've fitted in. Frankly I ..." But the elevator rescued him. "Sixth floor. They're expecting you. I'll come up and check on you later on."

The elevator door closed behind me with a hiss. I thought I was going to faint. Would be discovered lying pale and seemingly lifeless on the elevator floor. The red button marked "Emergency" dared me to press it. Madness was one thing — I was not unacquainted with madness. But an operating room! What did an orderly do in an *operating room*? Once, at scout camp, I had stood on the high diving tower, willing myself to jump off. I was so terrified I couldn't even remember how I got up there. I jumped in a state of mindless and whimpering panic, like a deer who chooses to drown rather than be chewed to death by a pack of yelping dogs. The waters closed over my head and for hours I fought my way back up through the oppressive water to the surface. It was neither an exhilarating nor a triumphant experience. Nobody clapped. Nobody tossed me a coin. My head hurt, my stomach hurt, my eyes were full of tears. I knew then that I was a coward and evermore would be so. All my upbringing, plus perhaps my own inherent personality, had confirmed in me a fixed belief that the unknown was to be avoided. Real life had become for me a street marked ONE WAY DO NOT ENTER.

I had thought this summer was curing me of that, but I knew now, to my intense humiliation, that I was wrong. I was just as afraid as ever.

Somehow I got off at 6. The shock wards were on either side, the operating complex straight ahead. Somebody, not Isobel, moved forward and knocked on the door.

A man with a disgruntled face unlocked the door.

"Oh. It's you."

Isobel came back.

"Who were you expecting, the Queen of England?"

"Blood," he said curtly and walked away.

Two kids passed underneath my window.
"Knock, knock."
"Who's there?"
"Sam and Janet."
"Sam and Janet who?"
"Samandjanet evening."

"Is it hot enough for you? Hot? I say, is it hot enough for you?"

"Have you ever *seen* such a summer?"

And still the rains held off.

Aunt Hettie was in the kitchen praising God and putting up preserves.

"Harry," I said. "Oh, Harry." And then, because he slept on, in the rose arbour, underneath his old beloved Panama, "Grandpa, it's Isobel. I'm here."

eighteen

Ruth and Lorna had gone to lunch and I was alone in the outer room with a pimply-faced student named Clifford, testing surgical gloves by blowing them up like party balloons or udders, then separating them into pairs, ready to be packed up and shoved in the autoclave.

"I don't know how you can stand this frigging place."

I gave him a superior shrug. "You can stand anything if you have to."

"It gives me the creeps."

"Are there any more number eights?"

He took a glove off the rack and, handing it to me, tried to brush my wrist. I had just told him I wouldn't go out with him for the fifth time. The operating room itself was air-conditioned, but the outer rooms were not; my hair stuck damply to the back of my neck and I was very cranky. We were behind and I was hungry. A great pile of instruments lay soaking in a pail of green soap and there were still packs to be made up before the two nurses came back. Clifford was a pain and I was glad when somebody knocked on the door.

But not pleased when I saw who it was.

"Hello, Princess. Where's your boss?" He had his arm around the shoulders of a big, grinning, drunken-looking man.

"Gone for lunch. They both have."

"Shit. Harold here has come to give of his good red blood for that op tomorrow morning. They're sending up donors. He's the first one. I went and got him special, didn't I Harold?"

Harold grinned and shuffled his feet. The nurse slapped him on the back.

"Full of the milk of human kindness, Harold is. Not to mention a few other things."

"Ruth and Lorna are both out. I'm sorry, you'll have to come back later."

"But I went and got Harold off his job. I don't know if they'll let him come back later. Works on the garbage trucks," he said in a stage whisper. "A dollar a day and all you can eat. Nice job. Nice job, isn't it Harold?"

The man nodded happily and shuffled his feet again. I didn't know what to do.

"You'll have to come back. I don't know anything about it."

"She doesn't know anything about it, Harold. We know more about it than the princess here. Now ain't that somethin'?"

He stood there with his arm around the loosely grinning Harold, challenging me, daring me to shut the door in his face. Clifford, whom I'd completely forgotten, came around from the other side of the partition.

"Who's this?" the man asked. "Your fella?"

I just looked at him, furious.

"I know how to take blood. I'll do it." His voice came out in a high squeak. Anxious to please. It was a bit like one of the Charles Atlas ads, the little guy placating the big guy.

I shook my head. "I don't think Ruth would like that."

"Why not?" He was all excited about the idea now. "We'll have it all done by the time she gets back. She'll probably thank us."

I knew in my heart she wouldn't thank us. I knew she wouldn't like it at all. The whole idea sickened me: taking blood from an idiot. *He* obviously didn't have a choice. Good old Harold. Like a puppy. Wagging his tail because somebody patted him. And yet, and yet ...

"I don't know what to say."

"Don't say anything. Just do as you're told."

His masculinity defeated me. I nodded. "Okay. So long as you know what you're doing."

We led Harold to the recovery room, a willing victim.

"Hop on the bed, Harold. By the way," he added, rolling up the sleeve of Harold's work shirt, "my name's John, John Kristoff."

"Isobel."

"I know."

"Clifford O'Neill," said the student, unasked. (Very important and his voice down now. Getting out the bottle and the stand. Hooking it up. The rubber tourniquet. The syringe.)

"This is my pal, Harold Rachman. You're my pal, aren't you, Harold, you old bugger?"

Harold smiled and gave a thick, muttering assent.

"What's the matter with him?"

"Your boyfriend should be able to tell you. What's the matter with him, Crawford?"

"Clifford. I ... Uh ... I'd have to examine him. I'm not sure."

"Not sure? Harold's not sure either, are you, Harold? Syphilis," he said to me, wagging a finger. "General paresis caused by syphilis. Let that be a lesson to you. Let that be a lesson to us all."

Clifford swabbed the man's arm with alcohol, put on the tourniquet, plunged the needle in. I had to will myself to stay in the room. Harold began to whimper and John patted his knee.

"It's okay, old buddy, it's going to be okay."

I made the mistake of looking at the receiving bottle, which was slowly filling up with blood. Harold's blood. Did he really know what we were doing to him? Hadn't it all turned into a game to impress me? I was awfully hot and sweaty and the three men seemed very far away.

Wasn't aware that I had fainted until I came to on the floor with John above me, sponging my face with a wet towel. There were great scarlet blooms of blood on the walls, the bed sheets, everywhere.

"So the princess is human after all," he said, but in a gentle voice. "You scared poor Clifford so much he knocked the stand over and pulled the plug out and spattered poor Harold all over the place."

"Don't." I had to shut my eyes again.

"All right, I won't. We were stupid, all of us. I don't think Clifford really knew what the hell he was up to."

"Where is he?" Not that I cared. I never wanted to see him, any of them, again.

"In the can. Being sick, I guess."

Harold, waxy-faced, was lying flat out on the bed, giving a little whimper now and then.

"Ruth, Lorna, they left me in charge ..."

"Don't worry. If there's any blame I'll take it. Harold's okay, but we better clean the place up — it looks like a slaughter-house. He pulled me to my feet.

"All I really want to do," he said, "is kiss you. But I need my job and I expect that you do too or you wouldn't be working in a place like this. Let's get busy."

A very sweaty-faced Clifford joined us, and in a dream I helped them scrub the walls, change linen, restore order to the little room.

"What about Harold?"

"I'll just have to bring him up again."

"You can't!"

"What else can we do? Clifford didn't get more than a quarter of a pint before you keeled over anyway. It's not going to kill the old boy to give a little bit more than normally required."

"I think we should tell Mrs. Goldstein."

"A pig's ass we should! I'll just bring Harold back tomorrow morning. It's the only thing to do." He put his arm around Harold, who was slumped against the wall.

"We'll come back tomorrow, huh, Harold? Have another go? Fun and games?"

They got out of the ward and into the elevator just before the two OR nurses returned.

"Anything happen?"

I was doing up a pack and counting sponges.

"Nothing except a fellow from ninety-nine came by with a blood donor. He said it was for an operation tomorrow morning."

"Damn. It was. What did you tell him?"

"To come back early tomorrow morning if you didn't phone him up."

"Good girl."

Clifford was very busy with the rubber gloves.

John Kristoff came up very early the next morning and I stayed well away. It was poor Clifford who had to go down the hall with Ruth "to see how it's done." I was furious with John and him but especially with myself. At my lunch break I went down to 88 to confess. Mrs. Kolodzy was out and Mrs. Reynolds was writing in the daybook.

"Remember Aggie?"

"Of course."

"She died this morning, poor soul. We thought of nipping up to get you, seeing as how you've never seen a dead person, and God knows she wasn't sorry to go."

I burst into tears.

"Here, Isobel. That's not like you. Tell Mama what's the matter."

"Knock, knock."
"Who's there?"
"Jenny."
"Jenny who?"
"Jennytalia."

At first Isobel did not dare to go beyond the swinging doors until the inert shape beneath the blankets had been wheeled away. What held her back was the fear of what she might see beyond, a leg half off, say, or an abdomen being slit open as smoothly as an envelope. Maybe a heart beating naked in a doctor's hand. Later, encouraged by the nurses, she grew more bold, became accustomed to the new routine, the silence, the ethery smell. Those who came in for lobotomies had shaved heads, like convicts. The surgeon drew on their skulls with a red grease pencil. Drilled a tiny hole just here, just there, as sure of the place to stick in his tiny knife as a man who is witching water.

"That's it. Let's go."

And the poor mad thing beneath his hands, babbling of some remembered scene.

"Daisies, yes, daisies. Big ones, big as your fist. And Creeping Charlie! Oh! Daisies."

"And don't forget your hat."

"*Oh, Doctor.*"

"Daisies and marsh marigold."

"This one's a poet, for chrissake!"

"Isobel, come over here and give us a hand."

"*OH.*"

"Hello, Isobel."

"Hello." (Keep walking.)

"We don't see you at lunch any more."

(Keep walking.)

"What've you got there?"

"A leg."

"You're kidding."

"No, I'm not. I'm taking it to the lab." (Keep walking.)

"Could we go out some night?"

"No."

"D'you still blame me for what happened?"

"Yes. No. It doesn't matter. Go away, John. I don't want to talk to you."

He shrugged and walked away.

The surgeon had written on the package, in red ink, DO NOT OPEN UNTIL CHRISTMAS.

And still it didn't rain.

("Isobel, there is nothing in life worth clenching your fists about.")

nineteen

Fate usually catches up with us one way or another. It's just that for some of us it seems to take a little longer. I had ten more days to go on the Hill, was still working in the OR and still missing the humanity of 88, however sordid, but by now very interested in the order that the two nurses, Ruth and Lorna, and the various surgeons created between them. Watching operations became like watching a ballet. There was such timing, such precision, such control. I, who had lived most of my life in chaos and disorder and who had found on 88 a kind of undistorted mirror image of the madness of my family, found in the OR a beauty and self-control that was created out of pain and ugliness and decay. Outside of the operating room the doctors told coarse jokes or exchanged golf scores, drank coffee, smoked cigarettes, pinched my bottom. Inside they were translated into gods.

And the nurses, pleased at my interest, explained, demonstrated, invited me in for a closer look. It did not disturb me (then) that I saw the bodies which lay beneath the sheets as merely a breast to be removed, a hip to be pinned, a brain to be disconnected or rearranged.

It rained the night before I finally lost my virginity. Rained buckets, torrents, cats and dogs. Started at seven and didn't let up until nearly dawn. Little kids danced in the shining streets in their bathing suits until their mothers yelled at them to come in for bed. You could almost hear the parched earth gulping, gulping.

I sat on the porch with my parents.

"There's a lot of farmers'll appreciate that," said my father. The air was fresh and cool and the sound of the falling rain was soothing. Jane came out and joined us. She had been writing letters in her room and sat with them in her lap, waiting for the rain to let up a little so she could run down to the corner and post them. We were not exactly what you'd call a *family*, but there we all were on the porch, together, father, mother, daughters, dog, all drinking in the rain. I look back on that moment as something very rare and very special.

The next afternoon I cut my finger open with a scalpel blade. It happened so quickly that I didn't really take it in, just stared dumbly at this bleeding hand which emerged, after a sharp stab of pain, from the soapy water. There was a deep gash just underneath my thumbnail. Right down to the bone. I pressed some sponges on it but it didn't stop bleeding. Ruth and Lorna were out to lunch, of course, and I was all alone. My first reaction — besides pain — was anger. The doctors were supposed to remove the scalpel blades and put them in a separate basin; to leave one still in the handle was a careless and dangerous act.

The damn thing wouldn't stop bleeding.

I began to feel very frightened, alone there with my bloody hand, which was beginning to throb terribly. Ruth and Lorna wouldn't be back for ages. I sat on a chair with my head between my knees, trying not to faint.

Eventually I got up drunkenly and went out the door, crossing over to 99, where I knew John Kristoff worked. I knocked on the door with my good hand. Nobody came. I knocked again, louder. After a long time one of the other wise guys who teased me on the elevator opened the door and looked at me in surprise.

"What have we here? What's the matter, Princess, have you finally broken down and decided to grant us your favours?"

Men in shabby dressing gowns and carpet slippers crowded and snuffled behind him, eager to be part of this new thing.

"Please," I said, "I've hurt my hand. It won't stop bleeding." I held it out like an offering.

He unwound the towel and whistled.

"Christ! How did you manage to do that?"

"On a knife blade. Nobody's there."

"C'mon," he said, supporting me, "we'll fix you up. You're lucky if you didn't cut the nerve."

The corridor became a great aquarium. Faces came and went in front of me. Stitches. Shots. All the things I'd watched with such aplomb until today. The sweet smell of gangrene. My finger turning dead and falling off.

From a long way away Isobel asked him what he was going to do.

"Fix it up. You can't just leave it hanging open like that."

I threw up all over his shoes.

He hauled me into the nurses' station, sat me down on a stool and gave me a drink of water and a pill.

"What is it?"

"Never mind."

While the men crowded around the little doorway he swiftly cleaned my thumb, gave me a shot and made what he told me was a "butterfly bandage."

"No stitches?"

"I can't do 'em. This may be enough." Grey faces, bright eyes, studied me from the door.

"What is it?"

"A lady."

"Don't shove."

"Oh, Jesus."

"Shut up."

"You shut up."

And then John Kristoff towering above them, looking surprised.

"Hello, Isobel, what've you been doing to yourself?"

"Get lost, Kristoff. She's mine."

"Not any more she isn't," he said. "You stink. Go take a bath."

The men cackled at this.

"Go take a bath Louie, you heard him, go take a bath."

So that somehow he was gone and John Kristoff had taken his place and was sitting on the chair beside me. Whatever was in that pill it was beginning to take effect. I smiled benignly at him and related, in a very incoherent fashion, what had happened.

"So even the great doctors get careless. Does it hurt?"

"Terribly." (The freezing was wearing off.)

"I'll get you something." And gave me another pill, the same colour, which I accepted without telling him about the first.

We sat looking at each other; the other nurse had gone to clean up or gone back out on the ward.

"I've been by your house about ten times, trying to get up the nerve to come and talk to you."

"How did you know where I lived?"

"I looked it up."

"*I* never saw you."

"I know. I made damn sure of that."

I sat looking down at my hand, which seemed to be about ten times its normal size and had assumed a curious throbbing existence of its own. The second pill had made me even more detached than before. One man, who hadn't gone out with the others, sat at our feet, utterly motionless, his head cocked up as though he were really listening. It struck me as so comical I started to laugh.

And couldn't stop laughing. Laughed and laughed while John Kristoff stared at me in amazement and then began to laugh himself.

"C'mon. I'd better take you back to your ward." Still shaking with laughter, he half led, half dragged me back to the operating room. I sat on a chair again while he tidied things up.

"Why did you come here, Isobel?"

"I wanted a summer job. I wanted to get away."

"You wanted to get away?" And that struck us as so funny that we started to laugh again. And were still laughing when the nurses came back and John explained to them what had happened. I was utterly beyond caring. The afternoon had taken on an air of high adventure.

"Jesus Christ, Isobel," Ruth said. "One of those women this morning had syphilis!"

I laughed even harder at this. "Let that be a lesson to you." I wagged my finger at her. "Let that be a lesson to us all."

She went off to telephone.

Lorna looked at me with amazement. "What's with her?"

"Bennies," John said.

"Oh."

"A dope addict," I said. "A syphilitic dope addict. Hello, Mother. Don't forget I love you." Grabbing an imaginary microphone.

"Isobel," Ruth said, coming back very worried. "You'll have to have a Wassermann test later on."

That sent me off in another gale of laughter.

"And how," I asked, gasping, "how will I explain that to the girls at Smith?"

"Take her home," she said to John. "Take her home and make sure she gets home."

I went off on his arm, laughing.

We didn't go home, of course. When we got in the car I was suddenly sobered and we looked at each other without a word. He nodded and turned left, out of town, at the bottom of the Hill. We stopped only to pick up a bag of party ice. He shook some out and wrapped it in his handkerchief.

"Keep this on your thumb."

We drove and drove, my head on his shoulder, my heart pounding madly, never saying a word. On and on past fields of buckwheat and fields of corn, past roadside stands with pyramids

of tomatoes and crookneck squash. Blueberries. ANGLE-
WORMS, PUREBRED SPRINGER SPANIELS.

And turned off onto a dirt road he didn't even have to stop
and look for.

"I don't have a blanket," he said.

"It doesn't matter."

Tore off our clothes and smiled at each other. Lay down in a
field still wet from last night's rain.

There were no preliminaries. No endearments or kissing or
caresses. I just opened my legs and he thrust himself into me.

"Oh, Isobel," was all he said. "Oh, Isobel. Jesus." And I
thought, triumphant on my mountaintop of pain and dope,
looking down at the tiny figures tumbling in the grass, "So this
is what it's all about!" and began to laugh again for the sheer
delight of at last doing something that I had wanted to do for so
long and which was, after all, *pace* mother, such a slippery,
strange and utterly delightful experience.

"You have a dandelion," he said, "stuck to your ass."

I peeled it off and gave it to him, shameless, utterly wanton,
dressed only in a butterfly bandage and a handkerchief full of
ice.

"You realize," he said, "that you might get pregnant and lose
your good name."

"You realize," I replied, "that you might get syphilis and go
insane?"

"I don't believe it."

"Neither do I," I said and finally kissed him. "Neither do I."

202

twenty

Rome. Syracuse, Ithaca. Troy. I lay on my stomach in the sitting room, a map of Europe spread out flat before me.

"Isobel, don't you think it's time to start getting ready?"

Looking over my shoulder: "What are you doing anyway?"

"I want to go away," I said, "next year maybe. Soon."

"You're going away in an hour."

"I mean right away. I want to go to Greece."

"I thought you wanted to go to college. I thought that's what we've been scrimping and saving for."

"*You* want me to go to college. I wanted it because I never thought I had a choice."

"Working at that place didn't do you any good. You nearly lost a finger and you're more difficult than ever."

"I nearly lost a thumb," I said without looking up. And then: "Let's not argue about it."

She stood there in her old gabardine skirt which was safety-pinned together at the side. So innocent. So angry. Loveless.

Growing old. I wanted to comfort her — realized not that I had never loved her but that she had never let me love her and that these were two entirely different things.

I sat up and looked at her.

"Listen," I said, and then stopped, embarrassed. How could I tell her that she was wrong about things when essentially she was right. Life was cruel, people hurt and betrayed one another, grew old and died alone.

And did not rise again.

"Nothing. I was just wondering if I should call grandpa before I go."

"Yes," she said, softening, "he'd like that."

I went downstairs to the telephone. I could see my father out front, kicking the tires and worrying about the traffic on the airport road.

"He's asleep, dear," said Aunt Hettie, "I hate to wake him up."

"Please."

But his voice didn't sound sleepy. It came over the wire warm and vigorous, the old Harry.

"I'm just leaving."

"Be good."

There was such a long pause I thought maybe he'd gone away.

"Harry."

"Yeah. I was just thinking." Then: "Listen, Isobel, if I should die this year...."

"You can't!"

"I might. Hear me out, dammit, hear me out. If I should die this year, don't pay any attention to what your Aunt Hettie or your mother say but see to it there's just two things put on my tombstone besides the date."

"Two things ... What are they?"

"No regrets," he said and, laughing, hung up on me.

"But I don't want to go among mad people,"
                    Alice remarked.
"Oh, you can't help that,"
                    said the Cat:
        "we're all mad here. I'm mad. You're mad."
"How do you know I'm mad?"
                    said Alice.
"You must be," said the Cat,
        "or you wouldn't have come here."